I0557437

A Party in a Stone

Lark Westerly

Published by eXtasy Books Inc, 2025.

Anastasia Blugle believed she had found the perfect companion in Dequan. When it all fell apart, Annie threw herself into building her fitness business and befriending a group of women with one thing in common. They were all ex-girlfriends of Dequan Qin.

ANASTASIA BLUGLE LOVES stones that sparkle with colour—what her grandad calls *a party in a stone*. While she waits to acquire one, Anastasia lives an active life. Most of her friends have trouble keeping up with her.

When Anastasia meets Dequan, she seems to have found the perfect companion. Dequan has a territorial cousin and an obsession in his past, but nobody's perfect. He even supports her ambition to become a personal trainer.

Then something happens, and Anastasia sees her bright future crumbling around her. She still had her ambition, so she sets up her business, trading as Annie Blue. Befriending Dequan's exes gives Annie a solid sisterhood, but one day she gets a phone call from a stranger.

LARK WESTERLY

A Party in a Stone

Copyright © 2025 Lark Westerly

ISBN: 978-1-4874-4333-7

Cover art by Martine Jardin

Published by eXtasy Books Inc

Look for us online at:

www.eXtasybooks.com

A PARTY IN A STONE

A Party in a Stone

By

Lark Westerly

LARK WESTERLY

Author's Note

A PARTY IN A STONE is set in the world of the *Being Tamzin* and *Performing Pippin Pearmain* series, but unlike them, the fantasy elements are kept to a blink-and-you'll-miss-it minimum. It presents the story of Anastasia Blugle, aka Annie Blue, whose first meeting with Tamzin brought changes to both their lives.

A Party in a Stone begins in 2017 and ends in late 2021, intersecting Tamzin's story at several points. It also intersects *Queen of the May* and *Geese a'Laying,* but it can be read on its own.

Why write a companion book? I liked Annie, and I kept wondering why she was buying shoes in Lady Lane, who her brown-haired plus one was, and what *she* made of the various situations she observed or participated in. So here's Annie's story.

By the way, the world of my stories is very similar to ours, but it has a few differences. For one thing, the COVID-19 pandemic never took place.

Part One: Anastasia
Chapter One: Blugle as in Bugle

ANASTASIA BLUGLE, UNDERSTANDABLY, had an issue with her name.

She found it inconvenient to inhabit.

"Name?"

"Anastasia Blugle."

Incomprehension. "Er—"

"Anastasia Blugle."

"Anastasia Bugle..."

"Blugle."

"Blur..."

"'Blu' as in 'blue,' and 'gle' as in 'eagle.'"

Faces would clear.

"Anastasia Beagle."

"No, b-loo. Blue-gle."

And then of course they'd spell it with an E. Or, occasionally, a well-read person would wonder aloud if she was related to *Ernestine Bugle* from the *Anne* books and be pleased to have made such an erudite quip. (Surely no one else would have thought of that one!)

Her first name was also a challenge. Anastasia used to lay odds on whether they'd treat it with a C or an S. She tried prompting them by saying it ended with "Asia," but they usually considered that a political statement.

Anastasia took it philosophically. She couldn't blame them for the confusion because, despite her assiduous search of surname lists and etymologies, she had never found hers. Even Bugle was rare—more so than Bugler. Blugle just didn't exist.

She'd asked, of course. Her dad, Mick, a phlegmatic football devotee, said he thought it was a corruption of a foreign name misheard, mispronounced, or maybe misunderstood back in colonial times.

Anastasia signed into Bloodlines and pursued the tiny Blugle family back to 1799, when a man calling himself, or maybe being called, Aleksander Blugle had arrived unwillingly in Botany Bay. His name, written in assertive strokes in brown blotty ink, appeared in a few records, with his first name acquiring and losing an X, a CK, and a double S more or less randomly. That troublesome B had a large smudge at the top of the earliest representation, and Anastasia decided it had probably once been an F until a fly walked through the ink and got squashed en route. Or something like that.

Flugle *was* a name, though a horribly uncommon one, with a single living exponent in the USA.

Still, in the country of the blind and all that...

Anastasia gave up after this. She had an enquiring turn of mind, but she was much more interested in kinetics than in linguistic blind alleys. She reasoned, along with Mick, that if it was good enough for Grandad Petre, it was good enough for them.

Petre—*not* Peter, as he sometimes bothered to explain—had a Russian maternal grandmother who, though long-dead by the time her great-great-granddaughter was born, was indirectly responsible for Anastasia's name. Olga, she'd been called, but Anastasia's mum had refused that fence point blank. If a grand duchess had to be involved in her daughter's name, then at least it ought to be a prettily-named one.

Anastasia agreed. She wouldn't have wanted to be an Olga Blugle. Definitely not. Someone might have decided to nickname her Olga the Brolga and sung the Brolga Boatman song at her.

The surname would die with her, anyway, because she was an only child with a lone female paternal cousin who had married a man named Seaworth the year before and gladly taken his name. She *was* called

A PARTY IN A STONE

Olga. Great-Great-Grandma was posthumously appeased. Olga Blugle had dived into the life of Olla Seaworth with a glad cry

Anastasia was a good-natured child, and she grew into an easy-going woman. She counted herself lucky, because it wasn't virtue that made her keel even. She just didn't easily ruffle. Her fascination with movement and momentum took her naturally into the sports arena, but, despite taking a friendly interest in the fortunes of Mick's favourite footy team, she didn't much like competitive sport, lacking the necessary desire to win at every cost.

It was an easy segue into the exercise industry. Anastasia escaped from school, took a couple of sports science and a couple of pre-med courses, and cruised off to work in gyms and resorts and, occasionally, in schools while she considered her modest ambition of becoming a personal trainer.

She was working as a fitness instructor in a gym when she met Dequan Qin. He'd been waiting for Jezz Finchley, a strapping blonde who swam laps every Thursday.

Unlike the other boyfriends and partners who stayed glued to their phones, watched the swimmers with interest or appreciation, or wrangled children, he was using a jeweller's loupe to examine a set of antique rings.

"Pretty," Anastasia said appreciatively, looking over his shoulder at a milky opal.

He glanced up and gave her a friendly grin. He was blond, or at least sun-bleached, and there was something a bit odd about the planes of his face.

Not odd. Unusual, Anastasia decided. She found out later that he was almost half ethnic Chinese, but he didn't look it. The other half was Dutch, which probably accounted for most of his appearance.

"Engaging yourself?" she added.

"What?" His face went from amused to puzzled.

"I thought you might be auditioning rings for your girlfriend. Jezz, right?" She'd seen them arrive together.

He nodded. "Jezz Finchley. No. These wouldn't fit her. In any case, she's not my girlfriend—just a friendly ex."

"Really?"

He nodded. "Yep. We were at school together. She's a designer. Uses a lot of vintage fabrics."

Anastasia thought that was a bit of a non sequitur, but she soon discovered it was the literal truth and made sense once one knew the context.

"Dequan Qin," he said, offering a hand.

"Anastasia Blugle."

His eyes narrowed more than most when he smiled, and he was fairly beaming then. "Snap."

"Snap?"

"I'll try to spell yours if you try to spell mine."

"Oh." She saw what he meant. "Er—D-e-c-l-a-n... K-e-e-n?"

"Not bad."

She preened.

"But not good either. D-e-q-u-a-n Q-i-n."

"Blimey," Anastasia said. "I think you win. Go on then."

"A-n-a-s-t-a-either-c-or-s-i-a," he said.

"S," she said.

He nodded. "And...B-u-"

She shook her head. "Blugle."

"B-l-u-e-g-a-l?"

"No." She spelled it for him.

"Honours even," he said.

Jezz finished her lap and levered herself out of the pool, then came to drip over Dequan in a manner that suggested they were indeed old friends but nothing warmer.

Anastasia surprised herself by feeling cautiously glad about that.

Chapter Two: Wasserplatte

ANASTASIA WAS A BIT dampened when she learned, via Jezz, that Dequan did have a girlfriend. It just wasn't Jezz.

"We went about for a bit, but it was never serious," as Jezz put it during a water break after a vigorous step class.

Anastasia didn't ask why not, but Jezz told her anyway. "We were at school together, and Deq was seeing the girl who lived next door to me. Tamzin, her name was. She did Years Eleven and Twelve at our school and then the family up and left." She clicked her fingers. "Just like that, the day after the Year Twelve formal.

"She and Deq had been planning a gap year in a van, and he was cut up when Tam and her family flitted. By the time he came round to see why she wasn't answering his texts, they were well gone. He called in to Mum's place, but we couldn't help. Tam's dad was there a couple of days after she and her mum left, and he said his mum was sick or something. No, maybe it was Tam's mum's mum."

She mopped her face with the corner of her towel.

"Deq used to come round after that to talk search strategies and so on. Tam and I had been planning to go shopping the day she left, and Deq seemed to think there might be a clue in that. He always had a new theory. And eventually we just drifted into being a couple.

"We didn't last, though. There was always the skeleton at the feast. In the end, I told him I thought the whole search thing was getting unhealthy. That didn't go down well, so I topped it off by saying he'd be better off with someone who had never known Tam."

"Did he ever find her?" Anastasia asked more casually than she felt.

"Not as far as I know, and I reckon I *would* know. You'd have to ask his cousin, Lucy, or maybe Delphine."

"Who's Delphine?"

"Deq's current girlfriend."

Anastasia glanced involuntarily over her shoulder.

"You won't spot her round here," Jezz told her with a chuckle. "She's a drama student—looks like an ingenue from a telenovela, all Italian eyes and dramatic black curls."

"Obviously, you still get along," Anastasia said. She drained her water bottle and set it aside.

"Sure. He sources hard-to-get fabric for me. Trades as Qin-Find. *If Qin can't find it, no one can.* And I reckon he can find almost anything—except for Tam, of course."

Jezz took herself off to the showers, and Anastasia changed her shoes and socks, pushed her fingers through her short red hair, and headed off to urge some enthusiasm into a spin class.

Pity, she thought, as she checked postures and pedals before hitting up the music. She'd liked Dequan Qin, but she wasn't surprised he was taken. All the best ones were.

It was about six months later that Jezz unexpectedly invited Anastasia for coffee after the gym closed at ten pm.

They were both in their street clothes, which in Anastasia's case was a pair of blue shorts, a singlet top, and a cap.

Come to that, it was more or less what she wore for the classes, but having multiple sets of the same clothes made getting ready in the mornings a breeze.

"I don't drink coffee," she said.

Jezz looked thunderstruck.

"Thought you knew."

"A beer then?"

Anastasia shook her head, grinning.

"Vodka?"

"Nope."

"Some esoteric sports drink?"

"No."

"What then?"

"Water."

"Seriously?"

"Seriously. If I'm feeling daring, I add a squeeze of lime."

Jezz blinked. "You'd be a cheap date."

"I suppose so. Was this going to be a date?"

"No. More of a friendly catchup during which you might hear something to your advantage." She brightened. "I know a café where they serve a *very* rarefied form of water. The brand's called Fossmere. Heard of it?"

"No, what's in it?"

"Nothing but water, but it's...different. You know how bottled water companies spruik their water as coming from sparkling mountain springs untouched by human hands, unsullied by water fleas, and—"

"Un-shat in by possums," Anastasia suggested helpfully.

"That, too. Well, this brand really does taste like that. They serve it with figs and cheese. I suppose you don't eat those either."

"Yes, I do." Anastasia glanced at the big clock over the gym entrance. "Will this place be open?"

"Till eleven."

"We'd better get our skates on, then."

Der Kaffeetanz was redolent with the scents of fruit, cream, butter, and coffee, but when Riva Bless, whom Jezz mentioned was the manager, came over in her dirndl and Tyrolean shoes, she was perfectly willing to serve them *Wasserplatte*. "Celery with that?" she asked.

Jezz nodded. "And *kaffee* for me—if you don't mind?" She glanced at Anastasia.

"Not a bit. I don't mind the smell—just don't drink it."

"I guess you're quite hyper enough without it," Jezz observed.

"I'm not hyper—just—"

"Energetic."

"Right."

"Like the electric chimp."

"Oy!" Anastasia aimed a swat at her.

The *Wasserplatte*, when it arrived, had not only a crystal jug of water and two glasses, but also a selection of perfectly presented fruit, cheese, nuts, and salad vegetables.

Anastasia approved. She approved of the water, too, which did taste uncommonly pure.

When she'd cleared her half of the platter, she leaned back and watched Jezz scooping froth out of her coffee, which smelled of chocolate and vanilla. "So what advantageous thing might I learn? Don't keep me in suspense. I think they want to close soon."

"When you're ready," Riva Bless said, reaching over Jezz's shoulder to place a folded paper in front of her.

"Sure." Jezz nodded to Anastasia. "This is on me."

"Okay. I'll get the next one."

Jezz grinned at her. "I did hope there might be a next one." She picked up the bill and pulled a couple of notes out of her wallet. "As for the advantageous thing—I'm not sure. I'm guessing. If I'm wrong, just pretend I never said it, and don't act on it, okay?"

Anastasia nodded.

Jezz said, "Deq's back on the market."

"Deq—oh, Mister Qin-Find."

"The very one. Delphine threw him over for a Shakespearian *wunderkind* three weeks ago."

"I see."

"All civilised—you won't have to mop him up or stop him going on benders. But he's on the loose, and when I mentioned you, he asked if you were interested in Shakespearean *wunderkinder*."

"Not remotely," Anastasia said.

"He likes hiking and swimming and live music—well, here's his number." She took a bit of paper out of the wallet, which she'd left on the table near the vase of sweet peas. "Take it or leave it," she added. "I'm not bothered either way."

Anastasia took it.

Chapter Three: Klompen at the Gates

IN SOME WAYS, DEQUAN Qin was the perfect boyfriend for an active person like Anastasia. He had plenty of interests and a busy life as a *finder,* and, being self-employed, he could and did plan his schedule to accommodate hers.

He was affectionate and good-natured, with a family he loved, but in whose pockets he didn't live. He had a flat on Abigail Street in Gilchrist, a pleasantly leafy bayside suburb.

His parents, Lui and Lotte, were welcoming and friendly, though Anastasia never got the feeling they saw her as anything but a passing ship. Juliana, his grandmother, was a more formidable person, but she, too, seemed pleased to include Anastasia in any activity she wished to join in.

The only family member who caused Anastasia the slightest pause for thought was Lucy Tan, Dequan's only first cousin. Unlike him, she was small in stature, and she *did* look Chinese. She reminded Anastasia of a watchful small dog, always ready to take exception to any passing car, bike, sparrow, or balloon...or, in her case, girlfriend.

Lucy never said or did anything that could possibly be called creepy, sneaky, hostile, intrusive, or abusive, but Anastasia was in no doubt whatsoever that the young woman felt somehow territorial about her cousin.

Dequan called her Lucy-Lou, and often referred to her, included her, or just assumed Anastasia liked her as much as he did. Obviously, she would be at family things, since they shared two grandparents, but was there a reason for her to be sharing supper with them two or three times a week?

It crossed her mind now and then that Dequan might be using Lucy as a canary in the mine or as a bodyguard...though what possible threat a smaller, younger, female cousin could protect him from was beyond her.

Having pondered the question for a few weeks, she invited Jezz back to Der Kaffeetanz for another *Wasserplatte.*

They convened there on a Monday, when Dequan was sourcing agistment for someone's sheep, which had outgrown its owner's tiny back garden.

Conversation was general at first, but finally Jezz said, "To what do I owe..." and left it hanging.

"I owed you a supper, though this is a late breakfast," Anastasia said.

"So you did. So. How are you getting on with Himself?"

"Fine," Anastasia said truthfully. "I keep waiting for the cracks to show."

"He doesn't really have many, now he's stopped obsessing over his lost lurve," Jezz said. "He *has* stopped, hasn't he? It was—what—back in two-thousand-and-nine or early two-thousand-and-ten."

"Six years," Anastasia said thoughtfully. "And in seven years you can be—"

"Presumed dead," Jazz said. "I doubt Tamzin's dead, though. She and her mum did leave overnight, but her dad packed up the place, and a moving van came—so I don't think they went missing, as such. They just left."

"Without a forwarding address."

Jezz shrugged. "Weird, but it *does* happen. I mean—my mum has a brother she hasn't heard from in *years*, but we've got no reason to think there's anything wrong. I doubt if I'd know Uncle Oliver if I tripped over him. They didn't fall out, but my dad and Uncle Oliver didn't get on. Come to that, my dad didn't get on with anyone much. But Mum and Uncle Oliver's wife had nothing in common. Mum's so laidback she's nearly horizontal, and Christine is always busy-busy-busy. Just one of those things."

"Do you know where he is?" Anastasia asked.

"Oh, yes—place called Farnorth House. A convention centre. I might drop in and say hi one day. Or not. So *is* Dequan still trying to find Tam?"

"Not to my knowledge," Anastasia said.

"You'd know if he was. He's not the secretive type. No trouble in paradise, then."

"No." Anastasia ate a small bunch of grapes.

"What?" Jezz asked, grinning.

"Okay. I'll say it. What's the deal with Cousin Lucy?"

Jezz's face twitched and she started to laugh. "Ah! Deq's puppy!"

"What?"

"That's what Mister Miller used to call her. He was the groundsman at school. When Lucy started at Diversity High, she just homed in on Deq as her anchor and port in the storm, and I guess it's stayed that way. They're really good friends. Don't worry, there's nothing creepy about it. She's the little sister he never had. She'll be off on her ship soon, I guess, and out of your hair for several months."

"What do you mean?"

"She works for a kind of holiday camp that's set up on an island—FIFO, except she goes to and from by sailing ship. This is her downtime, which is why she's got plenty of time to spend with you and Deq."

"Oh." Anastasia tried not to sound relieved. She realised she had heard something about ships. She tended to tune out and step back, metaphorically speaking, when Lucy was in residence.

"I hope you haven't—"

Anastasia shook her head. "I like her all right. It just seemed odd."

"I expect she likes you all right, too. I can guarantee you'd know if she didn't."

"Hmm."

Jezz swiped a piece of pumpkin bread through the remaining mustard and stuck it in her mouth. "Is there anything else you want to know? It will go no further."

"No. All good," Anastasia said. She meant it. Jezz had no axes to grind as far as she could see.

"By the by, I like your top," Jezz said.

Anastasia glanced down at herself. "Really?" She tried to keep the scepticism out of her voice. Her white logo-printed top was like nothing Jezz ever wore.

"It suits you," Jezz said. "It's far better to wear what looks good on you rather than being a slave to fashion."

"But you're a designer."

"Very true."

Anastasia said abruptly, "Jezz, if I ever wanted to change up my style, what would look good?"

Jezz didn't rush into answer but considered slowly. "You look good in sports clothes and blue and white. You're a perfect size ten, right?"

Anastasia nodded.

"You could also carry off a draped dress—dark red would work. Not slinky, and not tailored but..." Her voice trailed off. "Tell you what. I'll design one for you. No obligation. If it's not *you*, I can wish it onto someone else."

"Thanks."

"You can use it to knock Deq's socks off—always supposing you want to."

Lucy duly disappeared onto her ship, *Robinson Crusoe*, bound for Camp Ferris on Ferris Island, where she worked as a camp companion.

She called round to make her farewells, and when she left, Anastasia cautiously asked for enlightenment about her role.

Dequan said it was just what it sounded like.

"The campers on Ferris live an early nineteenth-century-style existence, and the companions are there to teach them the skills they need and to sort out any dramas before they get started."

"Have you ever been to one of the camps?" Anastasia asked.

"Not me, Stace. I like my electronics."

"None allowed at the camp?"

"Exactly. They're left behind before the ship sails. Some people use the camps for a kind of modernity detox. Wouldn't suit me. They don't even have coffee." He laughed at her expression. "That wouldn't bother you."

"No." She glanced at the clock—a cuckoo clock he'd got from somewhere or other. "Better go, I suppose."

"Stay over," he said.

"Okay."

He half got up from his chair before shaking his head and settling down again.

"What?"

"*Klompen* at the gate...only there's no need for it now."

"Oh." She laughed. "I guess not."

Dequan had a pair of decorative wooden clogs which lived in a corner of the kitchen, except when Anastasia stayed the night, when he solemnly put them out on the porch. He'd been perfectly open about the reason.

"It's a thing for Lucy. If I have someone here, she likes a bit of a warning so she doesn't just let herself in. Hence—"

"*Klompen* at the gates."

"Indeed. Remind me to mark the calendar so I know when she's due back. I'll get tomatoes in to make spag-tom."

Anastasia got up and made the mark herself. It was a comforting four calendar pages into the future.

Chapter Four: Ghosts and the Life-Board

WITH LUCY AWAY, ANASTASIA settled comfortably into her life with Dequan.

Being equable by nature herself, she had spent a lifetime of being perplexed about the dramas other people played out—often unnecessarily, in her view. If one made a fuss about every tiny inconvenience, what was left to do when a big problem appeared? She remembered her grandmother saying how startled she'd been when Grandad Petre threw a tantrum over some bureaucratic red tape five years into their long marriage.

"Not that I didn't want to throw something at their smug faces myself," as she'd put it, "but Pete just doesn't *do* that."

On the occasion that Petre did, the bureaucrat remained immovable, because that's what bureaucrats are paid to do, but probably had to have a nice lie-down in a darkened room.

On the whole, Anastasia was with Grandad Pete. Make a fuss only when it's truly warranted, and people are more likely to take notice.

Anastasia hadn't met too many people like Grandad and herself though, so for a while she didn't know what to make of Dequan. She didn't want him to throw tantrums or to assiduously build mountains where she'd have made a molehill, but it seemed almost unnatural that he didn't.

He wasn't dull, either. He was quick-witted and curious, and he seemed to enjoy life in all seasons.

As Jezz said, he wasn't even secretive. She was sure he'd have told her all about his youthful love affair with Tamzin Herrick if she'd asked, but to ask details about a relationship that couldn't have lasted more than a few months, and which had ended seven or so years ago, seemed to be giving it more importance than it was due. If Tamzin and her family hadn't vanished virtually overnight, the affair would have probably faded the way most high school romances did.

Because he seldom mentioned it, or, to be fair, his relationships with Jezz or Delphine or any other past girlfriends, Anastasia let it lie. She didn't even try to get information from Lotte Qin, who might have been moved to wander down the family album track if she'd shown an interest.

None of my business.

Only...it was.

Aside from his family, the most obvious place to find out about the younger Dequan was what he called his life-board, which occupied a pegboard near his curio cabinet of oddities. The life-board had photos, a couple of certificates, a program from a school musical, a swatch of material, a pressed flower... All sorts of bits and pieces that seemed to date from his earliest years. Anastasia spent several thoughtful toaster-or-microwave-waiting sessions examining the photos in particular. There was one of a serious-looking Dequan at three or four years old sitting down with a baby in his arms... That would be Lucy. There were two posed school photos, and some casual snaps of him with people she didn't know. The ones that interested her most had been taken at a school formal, probably a leavers' ball, because the girls wore fancy dresses and mostly had their hair up. Jezz was in two of them, wearing a dark blue dress that looked much less dated than most of the others. In two more, Dequan was posed with a girl in a short green tunic-style dress worn with green tights. Her hair hung in natural waves, and she had a tiny flower—possibly a miniature rose—pinned to the dress.

"Tamzin, I presume," Anastasia said aloud one day when Dequan was in the shower. "And that flower is from the potted roses on the porch."

Elf Maid, Dequan had said they were, neat little bushes that produced neat little scented blooms in a peculiar shade of pinkish green.

"Now where did you get to?" she murmured, addressing the girl rather than the flower.

Tamzin, young, vulnerable, and joyful, looked up at Dequan with an emotion Anastasia could imagine without effort.

They looked so happy together.

Anastasia looked into the girl's face, searching for some sign of a problem, a fear, or a restlessness that might have led her to vanish a few hours after the photos were taken.

There were no signs. She looked like a happy, well-adjusted girl enjoying the social with her boyfriend and friends. She was on the threshold of adulthood but had a couple more teenaged years to round her out.

She was encouraged that the photos of Tamzin were pinned haphazardly to the board in a scrambled collage with earlier and later ones, rather than singled out and enshrined.

There were a couple of equally cheerful pictures of Dequan with Jezz and two with a dramatic-looking dark woman who must be Delphine. And Lucy... Photos with Lucy were a constant, right up to probably a couple of years before, when all the photos petered out.

There were none of Dequan with Anastasia herself.

There was nothing sinister about that, either. They had met about the time photos went almost a hundred percent digital.

The life-board depicted a cheerful, ordinary, happy sort of life. If there were ghosts there, they were vague and pleasant.

The only odd feature was the persistence of one particular shirt, which first appeared in a picture of Dequan at fourteen and continued to feature from then on.

Lucy didn't like that shirt and had often made pointed remarks about it. Anastasia would have had to admit it was shabby and had lost whatever style it had ever had, but she wouldn't have said so to its owner. He never criticised *her* perpetual choice of running gear, so it was only fair.

Jezz had finished the promised red dress, and Anastasia tried it on at Jezz's studio.

"Not with those shoes," Jezz said. She opened a large wicker chest and took out a pair of dark red kitten heels. "Size six?"

"How did you know?"

Jezz hesitated. "I have a good eye."

Anastasia got into the dress and shoes, and Jezz nodded judicious approval. "Nice. Not too girly and not too bland."

Anastasia met her mirrored gaze and felt almost shy.

Lucy duly returned from her months on the island and resumed her visits. The clogs—*klompen* in Lotte Qin's first language—spent most of their time on the porch. Lucy didn't have much to say about her tenure at Camp Ferris, because she said she wasn't supposed to talk about it. They went out sometimes to park concerts, and now and then Lucy showed up with a girl her age called Nellis, who had evidently served as a camp companion herself.

After a few months, Lucy went off again. Before leaving, she called for what she and Dequan referred to, irreverently, as *the last supper,* a ritual concoction of a home-made tomato sauce over pasta. She hugged Dequan goodbye, tugged at the sagging pocket of the shirt, which had acquired a few tomato pips and which made her cousin clutch at it defensively, turned to Anastasia, half shrugged, and hugged her, as well. It felt odd because Lucy barely reached her shoulder. Anastasia wasn't particularly tall, so it was a novel sensation to be hugged by someone and to get a face-full of glossy black hair. It carried the faintest scent of...what? Hawthorn blossom? How peculiar. Nevertheless, she returned the gesture and went to the door with Dequan to see his cousin off.

"Well, well," Dequan said, after he'd brought in the *klompen* and closed the door.

Anastasia turned to see him grinning at her.

"What are you looking so pleased about?" she asked, grinning back. "That the sacred shirt's safe for another few months?"

He waved that away. "You just got the Lucy-Lou seal of approval." He laughed at her expression as her mouth fell open in...well, something. He gave her head a rub, and she resisted the silly urge to purr.

"By the way, do you want to go to Winterwatch?" he asked.

"What's that? Some sort of climate lecture?"

"Would I suggest a climate lecture?"

"Probably not. So what is it?"

"A midwinter concert at Dancing Tor...just out from Dancing Creek. Know it?"

"I do, actually. I've always wanted to climb the tor. Grandad used to go metal detecting there. I went with him a couple of times."

"Find anything?"

He sounded more than a bit intrigued, because one of his interests was in collecting odd curios.

"A lot of tins in a little cave, and not even vintage ones," she said dampeningly. Then she added, "Oh, and on our second trip, Grandad found a gold-and-opal ring. He put it in the paper and contacted the police, but no one claimed it."

"Has he still got it?" Dequan asked.

"I expect so. We took it to a jeweller—Lawrence Goldsmith from the emporium—but he couldn't tell us much except that it was very similar to a few stray pieces he bought from a French émigré, but not one of them. Or something. I can ask if you like."

She thought of the ring, which was so beautiful she rarely did think of it. Grandad had said it reminded him of a party in a stone and that she could have it, but somehow that had never been followed up.

"I would like." His eyes narrowed in amusement. "Might even borrow a detector and see if we can find something ourselves. Would you like that?"

"What, finding rings?" Her imagination took flight.

"Finding whatever," he said with his charming grin. "So, Stace, what do you say?"

"To the concert or the detecting?"

"Either. Both."

"Yes," she said.

Afterwards, standing in the shower with water streaming over her head and swashing lather down her limbs, she thought she'd probably say yes to anything he suggested.

Though...Qin.

She shrugged. Blugle. Qin. Maybe she was doomed to a lifetime of spelling her name.

Maybe that would be a tiny price to pay.

Chapter Five: Winterwatch

Sydney and Dancing Tor June 2017

WINTERWATCH WAS A THREE-day festival. Anastasia had classes on Friday, so early on Saturday morning, they went for a run through the breathless chill of the Gilchrist streets, shared a shower, and were on the road before seven.

Anastasia would have liked to drive her sports car, which was, as she put it, *easy in, easy out* and a breeze to park, but they'd brought a tent and a metal detector along with a camp stove and fridge, so she settled for Dequan's ute, which he used for work.

"Thought you despised camping," she said as she cracked the window.

"No, why?"

"You didn't want to give up your mod cons for Ferris Island."

"Right, but I've got a genny, and this is two days, not four months, *ontbijtkoek*."

She smiled. He called her that sometimes, as a legacy from his Dutch mother. It meant gingerbread. That made this the perfect chance to—

"I stand corrected, my *smekh*." She didn't actively speak Russian, but Grandad had come up with that one for Granny Katie, who was a very cheery person.

There was very little accommodation at Dancing Creek, which was a blink-and-you'll-miss-it hamlet for 360 or so days of the year, but the area around Dancing Tor had been given over to vans and tents.

Anastasia and Dequan found a site and set up, then jogged the kilometre or so to the concert grounds.

A duo called Joe and Liz were performing folksongs. Anastasia admired their skill and their showmanship, which allowed them to turn a large open area into an intimate-seeming venue, but the music wasn't especially to her taste. She sat through the three-number set and the interval that followed, then through a group called Esperanto's Baby, whose vocalist sang idioglossia with a flair for conviction, and two other sets. Eventually her attention began wandering and she leaned in and whispered, "Do you mind if I stretch my legs?"

"Good idea. Shall I come with you, or do you want to commune with your thoughts while you do jumping jacks?"

He sounded amiable as he gave her a friendly squeeze.

Anastasia tossed up in her mind.

A woman seated on a rug nearby gave them a wave. "I'll watch your spot it you want to both nip off," she said.

Anastasia took note of her outrageous orange Indian print skirt, her motherly face, and the baby sling she wore. From the pinned-down front, a tiny, wizened face peered out.

"Pepe, my chi," the woman said, explaining.

Anastasia said, "Thanks—"

"Nell," the woman said.

Dequan said, "Want company?"

She did, but she really wanted to work out the fidgets, and she knew he'd come for the music. "I'll just go for a quick run—back soon," she said.

Dequan gave her a shove upright, and she leaned down to kiss him, then walked away to the edge of the performance ground and ran off down to Dancing Tor.

Twenty minutes later, she was back to find the woman with the little dog alone.

"Your bloke said to tell you he's gone for coffee and that he knows you won't want any," she said. "I think that bit was actually for me..." She indicated a vacuum flask.

Anastasia thanked her for the message.

The next set began—this time another duo whose blonde roadie introduced them as Courtesan.

The music continued, Dequan returned, and they spent the next intermission poking about the little cave Anastasia remembered with a borrowed metal detector.

They found more tins, a couple of stray coins so modern they must have been dropped in the last six months, and a horseshoe.

"No more gold rings," Dequan said, squinting at the dial on the detector.

"I suppose it was a very long shot," Anastasia said. She glanced up at the tor, a shaggy and rather rugged hill.

"You still want to climb it?" Dequan asked.

"What do you think?"

"That's a yes then. Let's go. I'll put this back in the ute first. I'm not carrying it up the crags."

"Don't you want to listen to the next sets?"

"We can do that later. They keep playing till ten, and there's all day tomorrow."

Anastasia gave him a grateful smile. "We could always do the climb tomorrow if you like."

A tiny shadow crossed Dequan's face, then he smiled. "No, let's go right now. We should never put off something unnecessarily. What if tomorrow blows up a blizzard?"

"I suppose jam today is better than jam tomorrow," Anastasia allowed.

Looking back later, she recalled the Winterwatch festival as one of the happiest times she spent with Dequan. It was a holiday from the everyday routine, combining relaxation and activity and the achievement of a long-held desire to climb the tor.

What would have made it perfect would have been metal-detecting up another gold ring with a dazzling stone, but that would have been a miracle, and she had better sense than to hope for it.

It was much better to accept the sunny paths life offered and not sulk because they weren't paved with gold.

Be happy with what you have.

Be content.

Live with gratitude.

And so she was, and so she did until the day she wasn't and couldn't be anymore... But on that sparkling midwinter weekend of 2017, that was still a way off in the future.

Chapter Six: Early Return

September 2017

LUCY CAME BACK FROM her island existence in mid-September. It was a particularly lovely day, Anastasia recalled later. She was ready for a run, containing her impatience while Dequan drank coffee and made notes for a new job.

It wasn't a waste of time—she had plenty of counterbalancing exercises to do.

Because he worked from a home office, Anastasia had to remind herself, occasionally, that what looked like a lazy morning routine of coffee, email, and newspaper-reading or quiet chats on the phone was, in fact, his work.

He was checking email when someone rapped on the door— no tentative tap, but a good, solid tat-tat-tat. "Are you there, Deq?"

Anastasia glanced at Dequan, who nodded towards the door.

She opened it cautiously and there was Lucy Tan, looking up at her with an enquiring expression.

Anastasia cleared her throat. "Hi, Lucy. You're back early." She glanced at the calendar.

"Yes," Lucy said succinctly. She stepped past Anastasia with a swish of her long skirt. It wasn't her camp uniform, which was reminiscent of a steampunk lady adventurer's costume, but a boho Indian print that reminded Anastasia a little of the orange skirt the woman with the chihuahua had worn at Winterwatch. Not that it was orange—Lucy was not an orange sort of person. She favoured green and...well, green!

"Lucy-Lou!" Dequan sounded pleased, then he must have noted Lucy's less-than-sparkling humour. "Oh-oh. What's put you in a snit?"

Lucy sighed. "Some idiot messed up the roster, and the director said I couldn't stay till the next rotation."

"Ah."

"And as my flat is sublet, I'll be stuck sharing with a sponsored student until it gets sorted."

"You can always stay here," Anastasia said, before Dequan could.

Lucy flicked her a glance and her eyes softened. "Thanks, Stace, but three's a crowd. You *are* living here?"

"More or less."

"About time," Lucy said. "Actually, I'll probably crash with Mum and Dad or Gran Qin for a bit while I unravel this roster mess. If I can. Even Augie couldn't swing it."

"Have some coffee, anyway," Dequan said. He glanced at Anastasia. "We're just going for a run, but you can mainline caffeine and fume over rosters till we get back. Charge your phone. Detox...or retox. Then we can make spag-tom. I've still got some of the tomatoes Nelis gave us in the freezer."

Anastasia said, "The run can wait. Sit down, Lucy, and tell us whatever you *can* tell us."

"Well, okay...but I won't stay long. Better catch up with Mum and Dad before Mum starts making aggrieved noises."

Dequan made more coffee.

Lucy stayed for over an hour. She was uncharacteristically prickly, even with Dequan, and twitted him once too often about his favourite shirt.

He said nothing but got up and retreated to the bedroom where he quietly changed into a white singlet, the male equivalent of the one Anastasia was wearing. Hers was the one Jezz had admired, the one that had her name serendipitously emblazoned across the front in blue.

Lucy eyed him sardonically. "Did you forget to label yourself into a matchy-matchy his-and-hers, Deq?"

Anastasia wondered if that was a backhanded swipe at her—but why should it be? "There isn't a sportswear brand called *Dequan*," she said mildly.

"Is that what yours is?"

"Well, yes." She smiled and turned up the hem to show the stitched-in tag.

"Coincidence, much?"

"Not at all. I spotted it and thought it was fun, so I bought a couple."

"I see."

"Stace's clothes, or mine for that matter, aren't really—" Dequan began.

"Sorry." Lucy sighed. "It always takes me a while to get wound down after a tour of duty. And three cups of coffee after not drinking any for months was probably a bad idea." She got up. "I'll go now...but I'll be back for spag-tom tonight if I'm still welcome. I pledge not to mention your clothes even once."

"You're always welcome," Anastasia said. She thought Lucy's on-again-off-again relationship with modern life must be quite disconcerting.

"Right, let's get to this run," Dequan said when Lucy had left.

"Don't you need to finish the email?"

"I need to run!"

They walked down the stairs from the flat with their arms around one another. Anastasia, buoyed up with the delight to come, peeled free and pulled Dequan's head down for a kiss. With her free hand she slyly loosened the drawstring of his shorts.

Then she let go and took off at a run.

She heard Dequan start running and slow down to deal with his drawstring. "You'll pay for that low trick, Stace—"

She glanced behind and, about to quip back, paused mentally as she spotted a young woman on the other side of the street. She was wearing a smart lime-green dress, and she had something on her back... A guitar?

Anastasia had an impression of brown wavy hair and hazel eyes, wide with shock and dismay.

What?

Dequan touched her shoulder. "Tag, you're it!" and they ran on up Abigail Street.

Fleeting impressions can sometimes make a deep impact on the mind. This idea nudged at Anastasia now and then.

She didn't encourage it.

Every time that shocked face surfaced in her mind's eye, she'd banish it. She didn't know the woman. There was no reason why the sight of someone out for a run should cause consternation in a stranger.

Maybe she'd encountered Lucy who, in her unusually prickly mood, might have said something cutting. Maybe she'd just remembered she should have turned off the stove. If that *had* been a guitar on her back, maybe she was a musician late for a gig. She'd been dropped off in Abigail Street and her ride had left, and she'd realised, too late, that she should have been in Abigail Street in Hunters Hill, or maybe Gilchrist Place in Balmain. Maybe she was an au pair who'd been summarily sacked by a wealthy family. She had looked a wee bit foreign...something about the posture or—

I probably should have stopped to see if she was okay, she thought as she showered after their run.

Then she recalled, relieved, that the woman in green had only to walk a short way to the Paws-a-While café, where Cilla Wilde, the warm and practical owner-manager, would doubtless render whatever help a displaced or stranded hitchhiking guitarist might need.

She put the matter out of her mind.

Chapter Seven: The King's Shilling

LUCY CAME BACK THAT evening, as arranged, and after the ritual spag-tom, Dequan proposed going to the pub. "I have to meet someone there about a job," he said when Lucy and Anastasia both turned to look at him in surprise.

"All right. I could do with a drink," Lucy said. She'd calmed down from whatever had been bothering her. Probably, Anastasia thought, she'd spent an hour or so with a catch-and-release boyfriend...or girlfriend. She'd never discussed Lucy's love life with her, or with Dequan, but she'd heard them use that term. She supposed carrying on a full-scale relationship would be difficult for someone who spent so much time living a 19th Century lifestyle on a private island.

The pub, The King's Shilling, was in Milson's Point, near the gym. Anastasia passed it every workday, but she had rarely been inside. Going for a drink with colleagues was less than tempting when she was on water and everyone else was getting cheerful, but in this case it would be okay, because she wouldn't feel the need to explain herself.

Dequan ushered them inside and indicated a small door off to the side. "I'm meeting my client in the bar. Won't take long, but you two might prefer the lounge. Do you want to order or wait for me?"

"Wait for you," Lucy said.

Dequan looked at Anastasia.

"We can wait."

"Otherwise, we'll be down to sucking ice cubes by the time he gets back," Lucy said. "You can bring us drinks in here, oh slave," she added in a lordly tone.

"Okay. Poteen, Lucy-Lou?"

She swatted him. "Cider. Some of the Treeve Perry if they have it."

"They probably don't. That's a Pear Tree speciality."

"We should have gone there."

Dequan flicked a glance at Anastasia then back at Lucy. "But the client wanted to meet *here*. He'd never have found the Pear Tree."

"What's the Pear Tree?" Anastasia asked.

"A lovely old pub in the park where they used to hold the lantern festival. It's tucked in behind trees—you'd never spot it if you didn't know it was there."

"Can't be good for their bottom line."

"Word of mouth," Lucy put in. "If they don't have Treeve, get me a Summercourt fairy port."

He nodded. "And some posh water for you, *bosbes*," he said to Anastasia. "Lime or not?"

Anastasia surprised herself, and probably him, by saying she'd have some cider, too, if they had any.

Lucy turned to her as they headed for the lounge. "*Bosbes?*"

"Blueberry..."

"Ah, the red hair. Deq's always been a fan of Dutch endearments. He's finally corrupted you?"

"What—oh, I see what you mean. Cider. No."

"I thought you were water all the way."

"I am, but I wanted a change." Anastasia smiled at Lucy's surprised expression. "There's got to be *something* other than water I can drink—right?"

Lucy said, "Do you drink milk?"

"Not since I got old enough to refuse with conviction."

"Well, we'll see. Tell you what, if you get cider and don't like it, I'll drink it and stand you a posh water."

"Deal," Anastasia said.

They sat down on a squashy couch, pleased to see they were the only occupants of the lounge.

"So, what's up with you and poteen?" Anastasia asked.

Lucy sighed and gave an unexpected giggle. "That goes back to my early days on the island. We—the companions—were still getting used to the rules and so on. It was coming up to New Year's Eve and one of the others—a bloke called Patrice—made up a trial batch of punch. I had a glass, and it tasted tame enough."

"And I take it it wasn't?" Anastasia ventured.

"Got it in one. Patrice said later it was basically cold tea and apple juice, but there was a spot of cider and plum brandy and some poteen he'd got from Maeve, his girlfriend." She shook her head. "No one got drunk. Camp companions have to be certified self-controlled...but inhibitions were shaken and, to cut a shameful story short, I propositioned someone I'd loved for years and got very nicely turned down. I was so mortified I swore off poteen for life."

"That doesn't sound *too* bad," Anastasia said.

"The man was my old design teacher from school whom I'd never realised was married with kids, so yes, it *was* too bad." Lucy shrugged. "Carrying a torch for years is a sad, sad thing to do." She grimaced. "You might say it runs in the family. I take it you know about Deq and Tamzin."

"Yes. Jezz told me."

"Good. She'd give you the straight tale." She frowned, looking thoughtful rather than cross. "I was pretty worried about Deq for a while. He was determined to find Tamzin, but he never could, and you know how good he is at following trails. Have you ever tried to give him the slip?"

"No—why would I?"

"Well, *I* have. He asked me to do it so he could test his skills. I was to go out for a day without telling anyone where or how or why I was going. He'd give me three hours' start then see if he could find me before six o'clock. I got a friend he doesn't know to call a friend *I* don't know to pick me up and drive up to Fiddle Bay. We caught the neighbourhood bus and just rode round—Deq was waiting for us at Borrowdale Junction.

"He found me easily, but he never found a trace of what happened to Tamzin."

She shrugged and twisted a lock of black hair. "They were just so *close*, you know? It's going to sound twee, but they adored one another. Tamzin's parents were odd fish, a mix of disengagement and hypervigilance, if you know what I mean." Still frowning, she added, "Sorry about the psych-buzzwords. Comes from the companion training."

"Oh? Isn't that practical demos about lighting fires and—um—weaving and so on?"

"Yes. We're also gal pals and lovely lads to the campers. It's a tightrope, being there for emotional and practical support while keeping it absolutely platonic and non-judgemental."

"How do you keep to that?" Anastasia ventured.

"It's a job. Besides, my unfortunate attachment..." Lucy didn't even bother with air quotes "...to Augie keeps me immune. As for the campers, we don't use our real names. I go by Nan or Amy or Jamie or...Lulu, say. Maeve is Siobhan, or Aoife or Shona...and so on. The campers themselves go by their real first names. No surnames, no personal information, no addresses...nothing to identify them to us or to anyone else."

"Does anyone ever slip up?"

"Undoubtedly. Not companions, but the punters do it all the time. They sign a chit to promise they won't mention identifying info—an NDA, too—but they *do*."

"What happens on the island..."

"Stays there. That's the plan. We can't actually stop them from swapping details. Can't even expel them. They're told front and centre there's no leaving until the ship comes back, and we don't have a pokey. The worst that can happen is they forfeit their bond."

"What if—"

"Too sad. Too bad." Lucy grinned suddenly. "At least, in theory. Everyone has a medical before they embark, and no one can catch anything on Ferris. Most of the problems are minor injuries which our resident medic patches up and mental adjustment ones which the companions sort out. Hence my unasked-for evaluation of Tamzin's mum and dad."

"And Dequan."

"Well—yes. As I said, I was worried about him there for a while."

"Are you still?" Anastasia asked.

"No."

"Why?"

"He's got you," Lucy said simply. "Jezz got impatient with him—not that I blame her—and Delphine was demanding. She loves drama, and it annoyed her when Deq wouldn't play into her histrionics. You're a much better match for my favourite cousin."

The Lucy-Lou seal of approval.

Lucy sighed deeply. "So there's Deq and you sorted into happy sailing. Now I need to sort myself."

"You're still—"

"Pining over Augie? Not now. Not pining and not whining, but he's still *there*. My ideal. I get along well enough with casual relationships that rarely outlast my shore leave, but if I ever find someone to match up to that ideal, I'll grab him so fast he won't know what's hit him."

"Even if he's a camper?"

"That," Lucy said with finality, "is *not* going to happen. It's against the rules. Existing couples can share a cabin, but there is no hooking up. Camp Ferris is to work on oneself, not on one another. End of story."

End of conversation, too, thought Anastasia, but she tested the waters anyway. Lucy was in an unusually loquacious mood. Anastasia realised they'd never had a proper one-on-one conversation before.

"Your punch-drinking experience didn't put you off cider?" she asked.

Lucy weathered the conversational switch like a pro. "No, oddly enough. We brew our own on the island, but poteen is strongly discouraged." She raised her brows at Anastasia and turned the tables. "So why don't you drink? An embarrassing story, is it? You propositioned someone? Threw up on someone? Got nabbed drunk driving?"

"No," Anastasia said truthfully. "I just don't like the taste."

They were still discussing food likes and dislikes and had got onto lychees, which Lucy liked and Anastasia didn't, when Dequan came in carrying three tankards in one hand and two bottles in the other.

"Treeve Perry Cider," he said, setting down one of the bottles with care. "They had some, for a wonder. Master Perry must be expanding his marketing."

Anastasia picked up the bottle. "I like the label." It showed a caricature of an old man beaming and holding up a tankard in one hand and a pear in the other.

Dequan glanced at it. "It's quite distinctive." He set down the second bottle. "Designer water, just in case."

Anastasia smiled and accepted the water in one hand and a tankard in the other.

"Here goes...something. Cheers!" She took a cautious sip.

Chapter Eight: Gemstones

2018

LUCY RETURNED TO HER island after a few months of reluctant downtime, and Anastasia happily went about her business.

She thought sometimes she was getting into a contented routine.

Work was familiar, satisfying enough, but not demanding.

She was lucky to work in an industry that paid her to do what she liked doing anyway, but an old ambition tweaked.

"I'd still like to get into personal training," she told Dequan one morning as she laced on her running shoes. He was already wearing his.

He patted her back. "Why don't you?"

"It takes a bit of organising. Business funding, advertising, venue, and all. And that's quite aside from finding clients."

"You'd go to the clients, so you wouldn't need an office. Or if you did, you could work from here. I already do. As for clients, mine find me. It happened organically, and I don't see why it wouldn't work that way for you."

"I suppose so. It might be risky, financially speaking."

She waited to see if he might suggest backing her. She'd probably refuse, but the offer would suggest an investment in a joint future. She'd do it for him if their roles were reversed.

"Probably," Dequan said, "but on the upside, you could get away from Nick."

She grimaced as she straightened up. Nick was the manager of the fitness centre. He was friendly enough—a bit too friendly.

I have a boyfriend didn't cut much ice with Nick.

So? You're not engaged or anything...

There was never anything to formally complain about, but some of the women wore what they called *defensive jewellery*.

"Nothing like a diamond sparkler to scare off the circling wolves," as Jodiel Eden put it.

Jodiel was also a black belt, which might have had something to do with it.

"There is that," she said to Dequan. "What do you think I ought to do?"

"Whatever makes you happy," he said. "I could help you to source info on grants and so on if you want."

She smiled at him. "I'll let you know. Ready?"

"Ready." He kissed her cheek and tweaked her cap. "Let's go, *bosbes*."

Anastasia brought up her free hand and snapped a selfie.

When she looked at it later, it was a classic, catching her smiling and Dequan looking down at her with affection.

"Want me to print it out for your life-board?" she asked.

"Sure!" His eyes crinkled. "It has a paucity of photos lately."

She got it printed the next day and brought it back to present to him. He looked at it vaguely for a moment before snapping into focus.

"Nice one!" He went to his life-board and shuffled aside some old scraps of theatre ephemera to make room for it on the board.

Anastasia stood back to admire it. She ran her gaze along the board, past to present.

Something odd struck her. Four girlfriends were represented. Tamzin was a sylph with wavy brown hair, Jezz was a broad-shouldered blonde, Delphine was buxom and dark, and she was a compact redhead. She almost said something about them looking like a chocolate box sampler...but thought better of it.

"What are you working on?" she asked as they made dinner together.

"Gemstones. I'm trying to track down a collection that went to auction in the nineteen-forties, resurfaced in the sixties, then got sold again. See?" He paused in chopping cabbage and woke his laptop screen to show her an old-style and somewhat faded photo. "This was taken for insurance purposes."

"What are they? Peridot? Too pale for emeralds."

"Aquamarines. It's called the Penstemon Parure. Ring, necklace, earrings, brooch, and bracelet. It's unusual in that it has an upmarket gold setting of the type more usually associated with rubies or diamonds."

"Aquamarine is my birthstone," she said.

He looked up from his perusal of the parure. "I'm surprised you know that."

"Why?"

"You're not much of a one for jewellery."

"I have a charm bracelet, and I used to wear studs," she objected.

"Charms?" He sounded interested, and she remembered seeing an exquisite silver charm of a guitarist in his cabinet of curios. It had clear lines and a lot more detail than most of its kind.

"Little old enamel ones. Tennis racquet, tutu, a hammer, a mortarboard, a harp, a paint palette, a stethoscope, and a rose."

"Odd mixture."

"I think the implication was that my choices in life were wide open." She smiled. "My godmother gave it to me at my christening. It had extension links, but it's too small now."

"I'd like to see it. It's a lovely thought."

"It's at Mum and Dad's. I'll get it next time I see them."

For some reason, that small conversation stuck in her mind. While rummaging in the box that held her childhood treasures and unearthing not only the charm bracelet, but also a rubber duck, a toy xylophone, and a friendship bracelet made of plaited wool, Anastasia found a chunky little book on gems and jewellery. She had no memory of it, but maybe it was a leftover from Petre's metal detecting days.

She took it back to Abigail Street and read bits of it in odd moments. There were far more gemstones than she'd thought, everything from clear and colourless to the peacock beauty of bornite and alexandrite.

If she ever came into money, she was absolutely going to treat herself to a gorgeous chunk of something or other... She remembered the gold-and-opal ring Petre presumably still had. What had he called it?

A party in a stone.

That was it. She'd wear a party in a stone. She remembered the dark red dress and shoes she'd got from Jezz and had still not had the occasion to wear.

Next time they went out, she promised herself. Not to The King's Shilling, or to Der Kaffeetanz, but maybe on their anniversary, if either of them could remember the date.

She frowned slightly. They rarely did go out, except to the occasional music festival or concert, or sometimes to Dequan's parents for a meal.

Well, whose fault is that? she asked herself.

"Let's go out," she said abruptly.

Spring had swept in, and there was a street party down at Cremorne Point.

"What—now?"

"Yes—now."

"Okay." Dequan had been in the act of opening the slow cooker to poke the contents, but he restored the lid, turned it to low, and looked at her expectantly. "Walk or drive?"

"Ferry. Cremorne Point. Street party."

"Do you want me to change?" He had on his disreputable favourite shirt. It was a greyish shade of eau de nil. It had evidently been green once.

"Well, I'm going to." She ducked into the bedroom and opened her half of the wardrobe. The red dress, swaddled in a linen dust sheath, hung right to the far end, and she pulled it out, shed her blue-and-white *Anastasia* top and her shorts, and stepped into the dress and shoes. It looked spectacular. Or silly. She couldn't say which. It didn't look right for a street party.

Anastasia slipped into clean shorts and a white halter neck top.

Dequan came in just as she hung up the red dress. "What's that?"

"A dress I got for special occasions."

"Show me."

She unswaddled it again.

"Nice colour. Not wearing it tonight?"

"Not to a street party. It might get spilled on."

"I suppose." He pulled on a maize-coloured shirt. "This do?"

She smiled. "As long as you don't mind the odd encounter with mustard or lime jelly."

"It'll wash."

It was Anastasia's white top that didn't wash, but she had such a good time it was almost worth the cost of the stain remover that didn't properly work.

Chapter Nine: New Year's Day

2018-2019

ANASTASIA AND DEQUAN spent New Year's Eve 2018 quietly. Jodiel Eden and her fiancé, Foster Drake, had invited them to a party on the harbour, but Foster had come down with the flu. Because he was providing the venue, which was non-transferable—no one else having the relevant licence to handle the craft—it was put off until he stopped looking, in Jodiel's tart words, like a week-old lime custard.

Anastasia, who had bought a silver necklace from a charismatic silversmith down at the docks in anticipation of the party, was disappointed. It was too late to book in anywhere else, so she and Dequan made do with a wander along to the point to watch the distant fireworks.

January 2019 dawned brilliantly. They went for their customary run, then Anastasia showered and headed off to the fitness centre, where a record lack of members turned up for the spin class.

Nick, whose name so unfortunately lent itself to derisive nicknames—why *were* there so many rude words that rhymed with *ick*?—was in high spirits and suggested Anastasia might enjoy a little one-on-one session with the weights. "You can spot for me, then I'll repay the favour."

"Not today," she said and left the centre before he said something more and she might find herself duty-bound to complain.

She was half inclined to pop into The King's Shilling for a perry cider, which she'd grown to enjoy, but instead she detoured and drove past the Coffee Cup Ring Theatre, a quaint place that specialised in live music, community theatre, and original plays.

A PARTY IN A STONE

Today's poster was something so different she pulled in to a convenient park and walked back for a proper look.

The poster was a vintage one, huge, flamboyant, and discolouring ever-so-slightly.

Cult classic Elven Archers of the Mist, it proclaimed in gothic lettering. *Starring Hein Hoffmann, Hope Gordon, and Alain Barfleur as Renwin the Wayfarer.*

Anastasia stared with dawning delight at the stalwart yet willowy figures in leather jerkins and flowing gowns with long fluttering locks and moody sideways glances. Several of them had curving bows and quivers on their backs, bristling with leaf-shaped arrows. That was a nice touch. One was an implausibly beautiful young man mounted on an equally beautiful steed.

The poster was not a photo but an artist's impression, and the artist had gone full on gothic-rofantica.

Double bill—film then dancing, said a second poster. *Gold coin donation.*

Ah! It was a charity thing.

Cheered, Anastasia took note of the starting time and headed back to Abigail Street.

Dequan was talking to a client on the phone, patiently extracting information the client didn't seem to know she had.

He nodded his thanks as Anastasia switched on the kettle.

A bag of tomatoes roosted on the sink along with a packet of pasta, a hand of bananas, a bag of carrots, a loaf with a knife in it, pickles, and sliced ham on a plate. Dequan must have been hitting up the Gilchrist Markets and been waylaid by work while in the act of making a sandwich.

That ham ought to be in the fridge.

Anastasia put it all away except for the bread and ham and pickles, then glanced at the calendar.

The patch of wall by the toaster was blank. Either Dequan hadn't hung up the new one or had decided not to bother. They both used phone calendars anyway.

She poured the coffee and handed him a cup before making two sandwiches.

He talked on for another patient ten minutes then hung up and turned to face her, rubbing his fingers through his hair before reaching for the food.

"Good sessions?" he asked, chewing.

"Hardly anyone there. So—it's New Year's Day. Let's go out on a date night to celebrate."

"Sure, if you like."

"I thought we might see a film. Do you feel like a corny fantasy and dancing? *Elven Archers of the Mist,* it's called."

He looked—startled. Then he shrugged.

"We could go to a different film. I just thought that one looked like fun. Elves in tights. With prosthetic ears. And a swoon-worthy young man on a horse." She sighed. "He's probably old and grey by now."

He bit his lip, then said, "Whatever you like. You pick."

Anastasia, about to elaborate about the mad poster and the chance to wear her red dress, found herself unexpectedly unable to speak.

Dequan waited for a few seconds, then looked down at some notes on his phone.

"Well..." Anastasia drew in a shaky breath. "You'd rather not go out?" she asked carefully.

"Well... sure, if you want to."

She said, almost without premeditation, "Do you want to call it a day? Is that it?"

Dequan looked genuinely taken aback. Then he blinked. "I take it that means you do?"

"No! Not at all. I just thought you might. I mean..." She swallowed. "No. I'm easy. Quite happy to go on as we are."

The phone in front of him rang.

Dequan looked down at it, put down the sandwich, and tapped the screen. "Qin-Find—Lucy-Lou! Hey, I must have known something. I got a load of tomatoes at the markets. Thought you didn't get in until—sure, come over. No, that'll be fine... Okay, give it back to him and bring your own. You can charge it here."

He half laughed, glancing at Anastasia. "Lucy-Lou just got off the ship and borrowed some random crewman's phone to call. Okay with you if she comes over for spag-tom before we go out?"

"Obviously," Anastasia said. She felt nothing but relief that there would be no awkward evening while she tried to enjoy a ridiculously cheesy film and longed to unsay what she'd said. Thank goodness Lucy had rung...

But...his face. It had lit up while he'd been talking to his cousin. When he'd been looking at her, he'd seemed...patient.

Chapter Ten: Annie Blue

March 2019

ANNIE BLUE. THAT WAS what she called herself now.

It was a reinvention of sorts, brought on by a topple of dominoes that wiped out the life she'd begun to envisage for herself with Dequan.

There was no dramatic break-up, but the genie couldn't be put back in the bottle, and although Dequan was just as considerate and easy-going as ever, Anastasia couldn't settle for *considerate*.

The sunny paths of life need not be paved with gold, but they ought at least to show the occasional glint of mica.

Contentment wasn't enough.

On the night she dreamed of giving Dequan the slip, the way Lucy Tan had described it, and knowing he wouldn't find her, she knew it had to end.

The desperate search a much younger Dequan had made for his vanished first love lay years in the past, but Anastasia knew in the soles of her feet and the tips of her ears that if *she* vanished...

No, that was a bad comparison. He'd look for her. He would triangulate her phone or trace her rather distinctive sports car via traffic cameras or check her work and visit her parents, but he wouldn't be falling-apart-devastated and obsessed.

Anyway, she wouldn't do it, and she was shocked that her dreaming mind had even thought that was a solution. Emotional blackmail and manipulation was not on her menu.

She waited a couple of weeks, and when no sign of mica flecks evinced itself, she told him she was moving back in with her parents for a while.

He looked downcast. "Is this about that film? We could have gone after Lucy left."

The film would have been halfway through by then.

"Or she could have come with us."

"It's not about the film and not about Lucy, either."

"What is it about then?"

"It's about...a party in a stone, I think. Anyway, I'll see you about, I expect," she said, and kissed him goodbye.

It hurt. She didn't say, *it's not you, it's me,* although that was sort of true.

She couldn't even work out how the stone came into it. She definitely wasn't holding out for an engagement ring. Maybe the stone just represented the mica flecks on the path.

She said nothing about her changed status at work, but Nick the Ick encountered Dequan one day and must have made a crass remark. Dequan must have turned a soft answer, *Haven't seen her lately...* or *We're not together anymore...* and the fat was in the fire.

Anastasia gave in her notice before he said something unforgiveable and she *had* to complain.

Then she poured all her considerable energies into achieving that long-held ambition.

She shared another *Wasserplatte* with Jezz, who was disappointed but philosophical about the change in her friends' circumstances.

"You don't need mopping up?"

"No. I'm not crushed. I'm just a bit sad."

"Does he need an intervention?"

Anastasia thought about that one. "I doubt it. No. I expect he's a bit sad, too." She hoped so. They owed it to one another.

"Then why—okay, none of my business." Jezz held up both hands, palms-outwards. "Just one thing. He's not obsessing again, is he? Because if so, that could get dangerous."

"Not obsessing about me or anyone else."

"Okay."

An awkward silence reigned while the two women eyed one another. Anastasia knew they were both thinking of Dequan—the lovable man they'd both loved, and still did, and who had loved them both, too, and probably still did— just not enough.

"What I really wanted to talk to you about is image," Anastasia said, crunching into a young carrot with unnecessary vigour.

"As in?" Jezz shook off the subject of their shared ex and removed her light jacket—one of her own designs. It was severely cut out of soft navy denim, with random silver threads. It was perfect for a rather crisp evening in mid-March.

Anastasia leaned forwards and selected a handful of snow peas. "I'm changing my name to Annie Blue for business. New start, new image. I've already treated myself to a personalised number plate... Yes, I *know*. It's a ridiculous expense, but I actually *won* it in one of those contests. You know the ones—they offer a freebie to a random person in a draw and hope at least some of the others will be inspired to pay for one anyway."

Jezz had a sip of the very high-class water and gestured to show that she understood.

"Now I want your impressions on how Annie Blue, personal trainer and one-woman motivator, might present herself to the world," Annie declaimed.

She saw how disconcerted Jezz looked and went on, hurriedly, "This can be a paid consultation. I'm not trying to take advantage."

"I design clothes, not images," Jezz said dryly. "But for what it's worth, I think Annie Blue is the image you have already."

"How?"

"Annie Blue is a gorgeous, no-nonsense redhead with boundless energy. She inspires and cheers her clients without ever belittling them or making them feel inept. She's encouraging without soft-soaping—everyone's favourite gal pal. She dresses in trainers, shorts, and shirt and a cap. Blue and white are crisp and appealing, and being a fit and perfect size ten, she always looks glowing and put-together with no unsightly saggy bits or bulges. She's not so polished as to look intimidating. What she offers is attainable."

Annie was so entranced she almost forgot to chew. "Really?"

"Really." Jezz gave an emphatic nod. "You have the car, the image, the personality—and now you have the name. Annie Blue is on her way."

This affirmation from Jezz meant a lot to Annie, because Jezz, as Lucy Tan had remarked, gave it to you straight.

She left Der Kaffeetanz with a renewed spring in her steps and a celebratory bottle of Fossmere water donated by Riva Bless, who had overheard some of their conversation.

Jodiel from the fitness centre was equally encouraging. She suggested hiring someone to make business cards and a logo and doing it sooner rather than later. "There's a studio in Fiddle Bay that does fantastic work—very individual, energetic, and reasonably priced. We share an accountant. Want me to get her details?"

Annie nodded. Ideas were flooding into her mind on a tide of adrenaline.

Jodiel tapped her phone a few times and spoke to someone she called Dahlia.

Dahlia? Really?

After a few seconds she texted the information to Annie.

elfie@elfmadeart.com There was also a phone number, which Annie decided to use instead.

To Jodiel's obvious amusement, she called the number immediately and made an appointment with an artist—presumably Elfie—for three o'clock on Saturday.

Elfie, eh? *Elven Archers of the Mist* had been the beginning of the end. Now Elf-Made Art would be the new beginning.

After she hung up, she realised she'd heard the name before. Missus Greenhow, who lived in Gilchrist not far from Dequan and who knew his grandmother well, had shown them the sketches an artist named Elfie had done of her labradoodle.

On Saturday morning, Annie, with mild trepidation, returned to the street where she'd been so happy for a while.

Not wanting to pass her recent home in case she encountered Dequan, she'd arranged to meet Missus Greenhow at Paws-a-While.

The woman was there when she arrived, already seated at an outdoor table with tea and shortbread while her labradoodle, Spud, sat beside her blissfully lapping a wide-mouthed mug of something that smelled like chicken.

"Spud likes his puppa," Missus Greenhow said cheerfully.

She was a softly rounded person whom Annie thought was in her late thirties. She wore voluminous skirts and flowing tops, sensible walking shoes, and huge, round specs. Oddly, these didn't seem to magnify her eyes, so presumably the size was more for aesthetic purposes than a necessity of thick lenses.

"I ordered you green tea," she said, smiling. "If you'd rather have coffee I can drink the tea..."

Annie accepted the tea. Since her cautious essay into Treeve Perry territory, she'd managed to expand her beverage repertoire.

"I've brought the sketch," Missus Greenhow said. "My friend's coming... She has a wonderful one Elfie did of her with her chi."

She looked up and beyond Annie. "Here she is. I don't know if you've met Nell and Pepe?"

Annie looked over her shoulder as a woman in an arresting orange Indian skirt wheeled a bicycle into the forecourt.

She had a baby sling bound to her chest, but even without that, Annie would have recognised her.

"We've met briefly," she said, as the woman sat down, fished her chihuahua and a disreputable stuffed toy out of the sling, and raised a finger to a passing waitress.

"Have we?" Nell asked.

"At Winterwatch. You offered to mind our spot while—"

The woman gave a sudden grin. "You're the running girl, right? You got itchy feet and took off for a while, parking your...um...boyfriend? Husband? Partner? Good call, by the way. I don't even live with my husband full time. That was the arrangement when we got married, and it suits us perfectly. Both of us. He likes sailing, and I get seasick. I like live music, and he has a tin ear. And so on."

Annie nodded acknowledgment, since that seemed the safest response.

Nell said, "So, you live around here or just visiting?"

"I used to live in this street," Annie said.

"Oh?"

This was going to be awkward. She glanced at Missus Greenhow, who presumably knew already but who obviously hadn't passed on the news...and why would she?

"Dequan and I broke up recently. It was quite civilised, so there's no need to..." She trailed off, wondering where that sentence was going.

The women exchanged glances, then the subject of Annie's love life was locked away. Nell leaned back as her coffee and shortbread and Pepe's puppa and dog biscuit arrived.

"Standing order," Nell said. "Thanks, Cilla."

The server smiled and bent to rub Pepe and Spud behind their ears. "Refill for Spud?"

"No, thanks," Missus Greenhow said.

The labradoodle sighed deeply.

His mistress removed a framed sketch from her capacious bag. "Here's the picture, Anastasia."

"Annie. It's easier."

"Annie...and you can call me Pud if you like. Dequan doesn't, but most people do."

Good. She wasn't going to be...consciously careful.

"Short for Paulina," Nell put in.

Annie took the sketch. "This really is brilliant. So much life and movement."

"Here's mine," Nell said, producing a sketch of her own. It depicted her riding her bike with her head down and skirt swirling, with Pepe acting as a figurehead, little ears and whiskers blown back in the breeze.

Annie smiled. "Perfect."

Pud said, "Elfie's brilliant. She's our official club artist."

"Club?"

Nell said, "This is...or was...one of our regular meeting places, but mostly we catch up at the dog park now. We belong to a group called Dames with Dogs."

"No meetings, no committee, no fees, no rules," Pud said.

"There is *one* rule," Nell put in, grinning. "We *would* expel anyone who called her dog a fur baby."

Pud frowned her down. "We're just women with dogs who live as part of the family. We get together to socialise in a dog-friendly atmosphere."

"You can join us if you get a dog," Nell suggested, unsquashed. "Mind you, Elfie's a member but she—"

"That's women with dogs or with the committed intention of getting a dog...or even with the fond and beloved memory of a dog-gone-by," Pud said. "We would *never* turf anyone out for being dogless, because the chances are she's grieving and she *needs* the company of other dogs, even if she can't—"

"To get back to the sketches," Nell said, seemingly knowing all about it. "You just show or tell Elfie what you want, and she'll accommodate you."

"She *gets* it," Pud agreed.

Annie nodded. That was exactly what she needed—someone who *got* it.

Nell added, "Elfie is surprisingly eclectic in her work. She does custom work and some of it is..." She trailed off.

"Private portraits," Pud put in. "Very tasteful, very..."

"Private," Nell reiterated. "You can read all about it on her website."

Chapter Eleven: Elf-Made Art

THAT AFTERNOON, ARMED with directions and suggestions, Annie drove to Fiddler's Rest, the studio building in the quaint seaside town of Fiddle Bay, and arrived just before the appointed time of three o'clock.

The driveway to the pretty, white-painted studio was empty, so she checked her paperwork and her phone, enjoying the scent of apples from the laden tree in the garden.

Just as she was wondering if she'd mistaken the time, a van pulled up near her car. She caught sight of a young man with light brown hair in the driver's seat, and for a second her heart seemed to jolt.

Dequan.

It wasn't, but the driver had more than a passing resemblance to him, not only in colouring, but in the slightly odd planes of his face.

Annie turned her attention to the woman who was sliding out of the passenger side.

She wore a grievously crumpled lime-green linen dress, and her long wavy hair was draggled, as if she'd fallen off a boat or had been swimming in her clothes and dried off in a salty wind. She came over to Annie and smiled, murmuring something about running late. Then she made an awkward gesture as if to shake hands through the car window.

Annie got out in a hurry, smiling determinedly. "Annie Blue, and I suppose you're Elf-Made Art."

The dishevelled woman allowed that she was and that she'd had a mishap with a rogue wave...and then it devolved that she'd misplaced her key.

She turned to the driver, who had got out of the van, and who helpfully produced one. "Can you let us in?"

"So you keep a spare with the neighbour," Annie said. She took off her sunnies and gave him a good onceover, then she said quietly, "It helps if the neighbour's hunkalicious."

Hunkalicious? Where had *that* come from? Some place of unsteady rattlement, to be sure.

If the Dequan look-alike heard this impertinent observation, he gave no sign. He just said lazily, "Sure, T," to the woman's request and unlocked the door.

Annie, still as rattled as Elf-Made Art evidently was, followed her into the airy studio. "Nice place," she said. "Is your neighbour coming in?"

Elf-Made Art, or possibly, T, murmured something about coffee and going to the city, and the neighbour, whom she addressed as Matt, started banging about in the kitchen.

Annie refused coffee and ran through what she wanted for her publicity material, almost on autopilot.

It was utterly surreal, because she had immediately recognised Elf-Made Art as the distressed woman she'd seen so briefly on the day she and Dequan postponed their run for Lucy's visit. She looked a good deal less tidy, and she didn't have the guitar, but she had on the same lime-green dress, the same wavy brown hair and the same slightly *other* air, as if she'd lived in a heavenly place and had tried to recreate it in Fiddle Bay.

An angel who'd fallen from grace, perhaps...

Annie couldn't have explained why she felt this about the artist. It was just an impression. And Annie was *not* a fanciful person, rattlement notwithstanding.

How very, very odd.

It was on the tip of Annie's tongue to apologise for not stopping to offer moral or practical support on that day of their first encounter, but she couldn't say anything. How could she?

Elf-Made Art was not only the displaced hitchhiking guitarist-or-possibly-sacked-au-pair or disenfranchised angel. She was also Dequan's long-lost first love, Tamzin Herrick.

Part Two: Annie Blue
Chapter One: Duck to Water

Sydney 2019

ANASTASIA TOOK TO BEING Annie Blue the way a duck, proverbially, takes to the water.

Jezz had been right in her summation—the image of Annie Blue was there—all ready to be occupied, inhabited, and *lived*.

Annie *was* Anastasia, well, almost.

Even Annie wasn't quite sure where the line was drawn between her private former self and the ebullient new projection. Perhaps Annie was a bit more wide-eyed and ingenuous than Anastasia. She bounced just a wee bit more, and possibly she reverted to an earlier version of herself—a young woman freshly decanted into the world of forging a path and making a living.

Anastasia 1.5, perhaps.

Annie used terms Anastasia might never have voiced aloud, even if she frequently thought them and she kept her occasional hours of regret and introspection to herself.

She *came on strong,* not brash, but forthright. She was eager, and she met people more than halfway with a grin and a cheerful *good morning* to every cautious nod or smile.

Annie Blue was single. She lived alone, having moved out of her parents' place as soon as she found a minute rental.

The irony was that finding rentals and agistments was exactly the sort of thing Dequan did for clients.

Annie had debated with her conscience for some time about approaching him. Her parents were kind and accommodating, but at every turn she was reminded of Anastasia.

She even asked Jezz for advice.

Jezz gave it some consideration. "I deal with Deq quite often. As you know, he sources fabric for me, but I quite see asking a man to find you a place to live a few weeks after you left him might be considered a bit cold. It's going to make the break look—permanent."

Annie nodded rueful acceptance of that, because it aligned with her own feeling. "It *is* permanent. I *said* I was moving back in with Mum and Dad for a while, but now I've made the break, it's made." She sighed. "I should have been straight with him and called it right then."

"I suppose there's always a temptation to leave a window open," Jezz said pensively.

"Unless the bloke looking out at you from it is an absolute arse."

"And he's not."

They sighed in perfect harmony.

Annie ventured, "For one thing, it does spoil you, living with Qin-Find."

"I never did live with Qin-Find or even an embryonic form of it," Jezz said dryly. "He was living with his mum and dad when we were going out, which was not long after we finished school. I suppose you *could* say I saw Qin-Find in the sprouting wheat form..."

Annie surprised herself with a giggle.

Jezz gave her an approving grin. "Tell you what. What if *I* ask him about rentals? I'll say I'm asking for a friend."

"Which you would be."

"He might see through it, but he won't cut up rough, and he won't push it. I should think he'd be glad to help you as long as he doesn't have to do it first-hand."

"I don't know," Annie said. "I don't want to take advantage."

"Life is all about taking advantage with thanks and giving it with grace. Leave it with me. I have more than one friend looking for a place." Jezz held up a finger. "There's always Lucy's flat—she sublets that sometimes, but I don't suppose you want to go down that route."

"No," Annie said. "Too much like the window."

"I'll keep my ear to the ground, anyway," Jezz said, but in the end, it was Jodiel who came up with a solution.

Annie hadn't even considered asking her, but an invitation to her casual and largely impromptu wedding in the Fairy Gardens brought a question to light.

Annie, phoning her RSPV for herself this Saturday with *no* plus one, asked where the couple planned to live.

"His place," Jodiel said. "We practically do already. Mine's too small...too small for most people, really. It probably couldn't be built today, but way back someone subdivided and put up a granny flat, and when the granny in question shuffled off, they rented it out, then sold it to my landlady's grandfather as a job lot with the main house. My lease still has a good while to run... Don't suppose you know anyone who would like to live in an eggbox studio?"

"*I* would," Annie said.

"Done," Jodiel said with a startling promptitude. "Come round, and I'll present you to the landlady. She's my aunt, so I'm pretty confident I can swing it. She's no keener to advertise and risk lengthy goalpost-moving inspections than you are to hang about."

Annie felt luckier than she thought she deserved. The studio was tiny and inconveniently situated in the corner of a back garden, but it was *hers*...for the next five years at any rate. Jodiel's aunt, an ordained minister named Reverie Eden, agreed she was grateful not to have to jump through hoops with a rental agency.

"Waste of time. To the best of my knowledge, the structure is sound," she said.

"And Aunt Rev would know if it wasn't," Jodiel put in. "Who looked it over for you before I moved in, Revvie? Was it one of the Blesses?"

The woman nodded. "Torsten. Johan's eldest."

"Keeping it in the family," Jodiel said. She smiled at Annie. "The Blesses are old family friends—surveyors and builders, or café owners and managers, but they won't lie or prevaricate to suit Aunt Rev. Their professional integrity means a lot to them."

Bless, Annie pondered. She said, "Any connection to a woman called Riva Bless?"

"Cousin of some sort—Der Kaffeetanz, right?"

Annie nodded.

"There's just one thing, in the spirit of disclosure," Reverie Eden said.

"Only one?" Jodiel raised her eyebrows. "Are you going to admit to being a fairy godmother, Revvie?"

"Not *that*—it's another thing. Well, two." She turned back to Annie. "Debussy might pay you some unscheduled visits. She's used to going to spend time with Jodiel, you see." She dropped a hand to her spaniel's head and gave her a rub on the ears.

"I like dogs," Annie said.

"And Debussy is a lady," Jodiel put in. "She won't steal your sausages, though she might give some pretty strong hints."

"A rescue dog," Reverie said. She added, "And I do tend to sing hymns a bit loudly. Let me know if it bothers you, and I'll glamour it down."

"No problem," Annie said. She pondered the odd verb, but she decided not to ask. Why look an almost gift studio in the mouth? "Rent?"

Reverie considered her. "I doubt if you'll give me much trouble?"

"None, I hope," Annie said.

"Well, then..."

"What I was paying," Jodiel prompted. "Unless that was family-only, Rev?"

"No, it was trouble-free tenants only," Reverie said.

Annie felt a rush of relief. "Done."

She moved in two days later.

Chapter Two: Focused, Fun, Fit and Flexible

Sydney 2019

LIVING ALONE IN THE eggbox studio was fun, and not only fun, but also convenient for Annie. Now she'd cut professional ties with Nick the Ick, who probably had no idea his awkwardly nomenclatured instructor was now working for herself under a new name, she could schedule sessions at almost any time and with very little notice.

Having no partner to consider meant she could visit a new client for a see-if-we're-a-good-fit session while the iron was hot, even if it were five in the morning or nine at night.

Focused, Fun, Fit, and Flexible—that was what Annie proposed, and flexibility cut three ways—flexibility in mind, body, and opportunity.

Not that it was all win-win-win. Leading classes, as she'd done at the fitness centre, had some advantages. Attendees caught enthusiasm from one another, with competitiveness and a dread of looking slack combining to keep them working on their fitness.

It was easier to hold a group's attention by the physics of group dynamics, and of course the centre had provided equipment, venue, and insurance.

On the other hand, the centre had limited the number of classes, she'd had to share with other trainers, and there had been all sorts of regulations she hadn't suggested, didn't think reasonable, but had been obliged to espouse anyway.

Working alone as a personal trainer, Annie had all the responsibility, but she could also book clients to suit herself.

Many of them preferred to work in their own homes, but a surprising number seemed happy to convene in open spaces such as the Fairy Gardens at Windhill.

Annie experimented with Fairy Gardens Friday Fitness, where she arrived at six in the morning and stayed for most of the day. Clients arrived as and when they pleased to join in, paying either by the session or taking advantage of a discount that provided them with a fixed number of sessions a month. Many of them bought the basic package of four, took a *Fifth One Free,* then bought another five before reaping *two* freebies. The sessions were transferable, too—if someone couldn't use a prepaid session, she could hand it on to a friend or roll it over into the next month. The four major influxes happened at six-thirty, midday, around five o'clock, and at seven. Another modest showing happened at around nine-thirty, as mothers and grandmothers swung by on their way back from the school run.

The paperwork of keeping track of everyone was time-consuming, but Annie considered it worthwhile, especially while she was building her clientele.

All Annie's clients were women, some of whom brought their children, mothers, sisters, pets, or grannies along to join in or to cheer them on, or simply to make it possible to get to classes at all.

Annie also visited other women for home-based one-on-one sessions. Most of them wanted to be fitter and more flexible, but Annie thought some just wanted some friendly and low-maintenance company while they jogged, danced, ran, stretched, roller skated, or swam.

The Fairy Gardens made a safe, beautiful, and interesting venue, and although the rule of no motorised vehicles other than wheelchairs and mobility scooters meant the Paws-a-While van couldn't enter the gardens, Cilla Wilde had a pedal-powered version that brought in pre-made drinks and fitness-friendly snacks.

As Cilla put it, she already serviced the Dames with Dogs at the dog park, so why not the Fairy Fits as well? The pedalcafe, as she termed it, was small enough to fit on a trailer if time was tight or distances prohibitive.

Some of the logistics of running an erratic and ever-developing schedule were challenging, but Annie was lucky enough to have the services of Dahlia Pengellis, the accountant to whom Jodiel had introduced her. Dahlia, in turn, put Annie in touch with a solicitor who guided her through some of the legal byways of sole trading.

"Bran St Ives is a peculiar cuss," the accountant told her, "but he'll steer you right and keep you out of trouble as long as you do *your* part."

Annie thought Dahlia was a touch peculiar herself. She had a penchant for wearing clothing that was both tight and bright yellow, but even if she looked like someone who ought to be tottering out of a nightclub in leopard-skin heels and eyelashes like tarantulas, her advice was sound. She wore what appeared to be a kilo or so of silver jewellery and jingled when she walked. She didn't volunteer any reason, and Annie didn't ask. After all, she never explained her complete lack of adornment.

It was going to be all right. It *was* all right. Annie Blue was properly on her way.

The eggbox studio was, as Jodiel had suggested, tiny, and Debussy did visit quite often. On the whole, Annie was pleased. She would have liked to have a dog, but she didn't see how to fit one in to her packed-to-the-rafters lifestyle. Having Debussy coming to visit gave her something she'd hardly realised she was missing. The spaniel was a calm and peaceful presence, with adoring eyes, gentle ears, and a softly waving tail.

Reverie Eden was an equally calming landlady. Like Annie, she was peripatetic, taking her services to whoever felt the need.

Much of her time was spent preparing for and conducting weddings, most often in the pretty, rustic chapel in the Fairy Gardens.

When Jodiel and Foster got married in the most casual wedding Annie had ever attended, it reminded her of her own goals—to say *yes* to opportunities and suggestions and to make it work.

It even provided an opportunity of its own. Annie put on her red dress and kitten heels and sashayed into the crowd, half of whom had turned up in what she thought of as practical yachting chic, and the other half in colourful combinations of pants and shirts.

The bride had elected to wear her gi with its black belt, while her groom, with no sign of the lime custard complexion Jodiel had mentioned at New Year, had white linen pants and a blue-striped nautical top decorated with anchors.

Debussy attended, along with Foster's niece and nephew as ring bearers in retro sailor suits.

Surprisingly, Annie felt exactly right in her red dress.

She watched Foster lifting his new wife into an exuberant hug and sighed just a bit.

I'll have what she's having...one day.

Chapter Three: Taking Stock in a Storm

Sydney 2019

THREE MONTHS AFTER her first visit to Elf-Made Art, Annie took stock of her new life.

A quarter of a year! It had been a packed time, and she'd deliberately left it until now to look back.

It happened to be a Friday, but today there would be no pre-dawn Fairy Gardens Friday Fitness session. A thunderstorm had been grumbling around the clouds above the city since the early hours, shooting lightning and making threats on which it seemed perfectly ready to deliver.

Debussy scratched on the door at half-past five, and Annie, who had been awake and listening to the sky salvo, let her in.

"Everything okay, sweetie?" she asked.

The spaniel's ruff was damp but not sodden, so she must have ducked out for her morning business then run straight from the main house to the eggbox studio. She didn't seem alarmed or distressed, so Annie took her into the tiny kitchen and turned on the heating.

She peeped through the window towards the house. No lights were showing through the streaming pane, and Debussy was placidly licking raindrops from her coat, so she assumed all was well with her landlady. If not, her husband could deal with it.

Annie had a smiling-and-waving acquaintanceship with Didymus Eden, who struck her as being a practical and down-to-earth person despite his outlandish name.

And you're one to talk...

Annie got herself some green tea and concluded that Debussy had merely come for an early visit, or maybe a check-in with her new neighbour.

She'd discovered, without surprise, that Reverie was a member of the Dames with Dogs. It made sense that her growing acquaintanceship of strongminded, serene, and practical women should know one another. The club was quite extensive, and a couple of the younger members, Pet and Fetch, often showed up to Friday Fitness, along with their dogs, Clancy and Tips.

"So, I wonder if it's a case of 'rain before seven—fine before eleven,'" Annie mused aloud.

Debussy turned and arranged her other side towards the heater, steaming gently.

"Probably not," Annie agreed.

She didn't hold outdoor fitness classes in inclement weather. She doubted her reputation would survive intact if any of the Fairy Fits got struck by lightning, frostbitten on the toes, blown to Jericho, or dissolved in a downpour. Besides, she didn't fancy any of those fates herself.

She could always review the situation at eleven.

She put the information on the Annie Blue website with a suggestion to check at eleven.

Meanwhile, she could run through her morning routine in the safety of her studio.

She stretched and began running on the spot before moving into other studio-friendly movements. It was all so automatic that it was no wonder her brain chose to take stock.

Fiddle Bay Late Summer 2019

A PARTY IN A STONE

AFTER HER FIRST SHOCK at encountering the mysteriously-disappeared first—and presumably most-beloved—ex of her own recent ex, Annie had pulled herself together.

Elf-Made Art had been dishevelled and off her game, which seemed odd, considering the glowing endorsement she'd had from Pud Greenhow, orange-skirted Nell, the accountant, and Jodiel Eden.

The flapping about couldn't be usual, Annie thought. Ergo, either Elf-Made Art recognised her as the runner who hadn't stopped to offer her support, or else something else had happened to set her all on edge.

Elfie—she decided that was as good a name as any until or unless it came to *call-me-Tamzin*—looked athletic but when Annie proposed a run along the beach after they'd concluded their business meeting, she'd said she wasn't a runner. Fair enough. Not everyone enjoyed running.

Eventually, Annie concluded that Elfie was used to being in control of her life and her brush with a rogue wave or a tumble in the surf or whatever had really happened had disconcerted her.

No businesswoman liked being caught looking like a crumpled rough-dried towel, and facing a new client and running late after a mishap was probably quite enough to ruin anyone's poise.

It was also possible she'd been having words with the tasty neighbour who had given her a lift home in his van. Maybe he'd been responsible for the mishap in some fashion.

He clearly knew his way around Elfie's kitchen. When he emerged carrying coffee for Elfie and a glass of water for Annie, she had him witness signatures on the NDA she and Elfie signed.

Afterwards, she tried to read his signature. "Martin Companion? Really?" she pondered aloud.

"Matin Campania," Elfie corrected.

Annie commented on the unusual name, admitted to her own, and discovered Elfie had read *Anne of Windy Willows*, the book that introduced Ernestine Bugle, her not-too-far-off namesake.

"Now that that's done, why all the secrecy?" Elfie asked.

Annie explained, candidly, about her new name and her new life endeavour. She found herself explaining about Dequan, too—though she stopped short of naming him.

".... He's a really lovely guy, but it wasn't going anywhere. Once I made the break, I had a serious rethink. I decided..." She continued, before winding up with, "So—new name, new game. I'm going it alone, and I'll trade as Annie Blue. Catchy or what? Easy to spell. Rolls off the tongue."

It had been freeing to tell her story to someone who wasn't a friend or one of her clients, and of course it also offered Elfie a chance to come clean. "This lovely ex of yours...might his name be Dequan Qin? Because if it is, he's someone I knew a long time ago..."

Elfie said no such thing, but she looked increasingly uncomfortable. "You're not in any trouble, I hope?" she asked abruptly.

"Trouble? As in?"

"Danger?"

Annie laughed. "Heavens, no!" She explained the situation with Nick the Ick. She picked up her glass of water. "You do the same thing, right?"

"What?" There was that wariness again.

"Elf-Made Art," Annie said blandly. "The woman who put me on to your website said your name was Elfie, but your tasty neighbour calls you T."

Elfie sipped her coffee. "He doesn't, usually."

"What does he call you, usually?"

"It's a nickname. Not the sort we would use in public."

They discussed nicknames, then Annie explained about her break-up. She felt, somehow, the need to justify herself.

"We just went along as usual until we didn't," she concluded.

By then, she reckoned enough disclosure had been done, and they steered the conversation into matters of logos and advertising.

By the end of the appointment, they'd worked out pricing and delivery dates. Elfie had relaxed, and Annie, intrigued, decided to test the waters a little more.

"You busy next weekend?" she asked.

"I'm going to a music festival with a friend."

"Mister Hunkalicious?" She'd decided that was a pretty good label for the tasty neighbour.

"No—Nell Andover."

Aha, small world.

"Pity you'll be away," Annie went on. "I thought it'd be fun to get together with your neighbour—has he got a friend?"

Elfie gave a hunted look towards the kitchen.

"Never mind, I can see I'm coming on too strong," Annie said. The neighbour was obviously more than *just* a neighbour.

As she left, she said, "I don't blame you for wanting to keep him to yourself. Piece of advice though, woman to woman—don't take him for granted. No one likes that. And *don't* fish for a future and get pushed into a corner the way I did. If I'd kept my mouth shut, I'd still be with my ex."

"Do you wish you had?" Elfie asked.

Annie thought about that. "You know what? No. I miss him, but... I'm not just a reliable companion. I'm worth more." On that not-especially-original exit line, she took her leave.

Sydney Winter 2019

Thinking about it as she ran through a series of squats and lunges with Debussy watching with placid wonder, and rain and thunder competing outside the studio, she tried to analyse her ongoing relationship with the artist.

On the face of it, she and Elfie were not a bit alike. Elfie was probably a bit older, but she had a curiously *beyond* air. She still reminded Annie of an angel who'd misplaced eternity. She was reticent and self-contained, artistic, and, Annie discovered, musical... A violinist, no less. So maybe the guitar she'd carried on her back had really been a fiddle. She did not seem to exercise—not as Annie understood it. Their interests barely aligned, except insofar as they were both running their own businesses as solo traders. Annie could hire Elfie for enhancements to her business, but she couldn't imagine Elfie joining the Friday Fairy Fits.

Nevertheless, Annie found her intriguing. It would be interesting to be her friend, because, busy as she was, Annie spent most of her time with clients. She saw Jezz occasionally, but Jezz was busy with her design work. It would be lovely to have a friend to hang out with now and again.

She didn't mention Elfie to Jezz, let alone to Dequan. She wasn't sure why, but she thought it was probably something best left alone, at least, by her. Elfie wasn't hiding out—she knew the Dames, and Dequan also knew some of them, so what were the odds that *someone* wouldn't mention her to him at some point?

By the way, I saw Tamzin the other day—Tamzin Herrick. You were at school together, right?

If Elfie *was* Dequan's long-lost high school sweetheart, and Annie thought she almost certainly was, it would feel intrusive to ask, and it would be far too uncomfortable to poke her nose into something that was no longer her business.

Why had Elfie and her family vanished? She'd asked Annie if she was in danger, so probably something alarming had happened all those years ago.

Anyway, Annie told herself yet again as she curved through some sun salutations, almost touching noses with Debussy, who had lapsed into a downward dog, Elfie had evidently come out of hiding or stopped running and returned to her home state. Presumably, Dequan didn't know she was back, but Elfie could find him if she wanted... In fact, she *had* found him if that glimpse in Abigail Street could be counted.

"If she'd wanted to tell him she was back—to reconnect as a friend if nothing else—she would have said something that day," Annie said to Debussy.

She tried to believe it.

The sky fired off another salvo of derision. Annie lost her rhythm. Even Debussy twitched her long ears enquiringly.

Someone rapped on the door. "Hello? Sorry to disturb you, Annie, but is Debussy with you?"

Annie pulled herself together. "Yes..." She paused, uncertain whether to say *Mister Eden* or *Didymus*. "She's fine," she added.

"Grand. Revvie thought she'd be here."

Bang!

Mister Eden gave a rueful laugh. "I'll see if I can make it back without getting hit by a thunderbolt."

Annie returned to her exercises. She doubted very much if it would be fine before eleven.

Chapter Four: Move-a-Licious

Sydney 2019

ANNIE CONTINUED TO feel a peculiar tug towards Elfie.

Her real first name *was* Tamzin, or Tam, possibly, as Annie learned during another meeting to discuss a new set of advertising.

Fiddle Bay Autumn 2019

"Not happy with what you have?" Elfie sounded a bit uneasy when Annie made the appointment.

"Oh, very! But part of my brand is novelty and innovation, and I want to come up with new programs—things not offered by every second fitness trainer."

"Such as..."

"Let's meet, and we can talk about it," Annie said.

They made another Saturday afternoon appointment, and Annie went just as she was, straight from working in a park nominated by her client. It was a quiet place, with a cluster of mature European trees at one end.

"You wouldn't believe there's a pub hiding in there," Bette Mallory, a plump woman who walked with a cane, said brightly.

"Oh?" Annie did a couple of star jumps and a cartwheel. Bette set her own pace, but she said she enjoyed seeing Annie in action.

"*I* used to be able to do that—the star jumps, I mean."

"Maybe you will again."

"Oh, depend on it!" Bette swung her stick. She'd been in a car accident, and she said working was Annie was a lot more fun than the rehab offered by her health fund.

Annie turned to gaze at the trees. "What's this park called?"

"Officially? It's named Belmore Park after a governor back in the day, but the sign went walkabout decades ago. Most people call it Hush Park or Quiet Park or some variation on that theme because you can't hear traffic here. Quite an odd phenomenon, really. Every so often you find earnest bodies with audio equipment trying to work out the acoustics. They used to hold the lantern festival here when I was a girl."

"Is the pub called The Pear Tree?" Annie asked, pausing for Bette to catch up.

"That's it."

"We might call in for a drink next week," Annie said, on impulse.

"Grand! Why not this week?" Bette was evidently not a fan of delayed gratification.

"I have an appointment with a graphic artist in Fiddle Bay."

"Raincheck," Bette said cheerfully.

A little dishevelment wouldn't hurt, Annie thought as she drove north after the session with Bette. It might help to put Elfie at ease.

But—this time, Elfie was groomed and collected, welcoming Annie into her studio with a composed smile and the scent of pastry.

"I've been using up some stored apples," she said in explanation. "Do you eat pie?"

"Yes," Annie said.

"No qualification? Good." Elfie cut slices of a still-warm apple pie and put them in bowls.

"Is someone joining us?" Annie asked, noting the third bowl.

"Matin's here." Elfie smiled. "Something went wrong under the bathroom sink, and he's wrestling it into submission."

"He's a plumber?" Annie wasn't a bit averse to meeting Mister Hunkalicious again. She thought he was something *more* than a neighbour, but—she had a quick look at Elfie's hands.

No rings. Blimey—I'm as bad as Nick the Ick.

"No." Elfie hesitated, then went on, "He works at a music studio down in the city. It's called Wildwood."

Annie nodded, though she'd never heard of it. Dequan probably had.

Elfie said, "We'd better talk your campaign through before he comes out...though the NDA is still in force."

"He's not a signatory."

"That's right... He witnessed it. Still, he won't talk." She gestured to a couch, but Annie always thought better on her feet.

"I go to some clients' homes, or we meet somewhere and have a session on the beach or on a fitness track or some such," she said, "but my most popular offering is Friday Fitness at the Fairy Gardens in Windhill. You know it?"

Elfie assented.

"It's safe and free," Annie went on.

"I know."

"It's an all-day affair, weather allowing."

"You want to advertise that?"

"No, that's already running just fine. I'm looking to designing another *day*... A walkaround."

Elfie looked a little confused.

"Most of our workouts are pretty energetic," Annie pursued, "so I thought a *walking* day would be a contrast. It would work the same way as the Fridays do, but it would cater for people with young children or elderly dogs or bored grandmothers or people rehabilitating from injury." She thought of Bette. "We could work on walking technique or do movement to music...even marching...or walk relays— just about any variation. I want to work in some flexibility and breathing exercises. The goal is for *gentle* fitness, with an emphasis on promoting better health and sleep. We might even have lunch built in."

Aware she was probably babbling, she wound up, took a deep breath, and said, "What do you think?"

"It sounds different, all right," Elfie said.

"You don't think it will work?"

"I don't know. It's not my area, but might you work in a bit of simple dance?"

"Yes!" Annie had to restrain herself from turning a handspring. Elfie *got* it.

"Everyone can work at their own level and do as much as they like," Annie went on. "So how do we spin *that?*"

Elfie opened a drawer under her table and pulled out a sketch block and pencils. She started sketching.

Annie watched for a while, then wandered away and looked out at the apple trees, bare now except for a few yellowed leaves still fluttering from twigs.

Someone came into the room, and she turned to see the neighbour—Mister Hunkalicious himself. He still reminded her a bit of Dequan. He was about the same height and build, though his hair was a shade darker. His skin tone was similar, and the set of his eyes and cheekbones were—oops!

Aware she was staring, she caught his eye. He grinned at her. "Hello...Annie, right?"

"Yes. Have you sorted out the plumbing?"

"I trust so."

"Let's hope so. Bathroom floods are the pits."

That seemed to be that. They both watched Elfie sketching rapidly. "Tam."

She lifted her head, and her eyes flicked sideways in what might have been a warning. Then she smiled. "You finished! Can you stay for some pie?"

"I'll have to have it now," he said. "Tezza has summoned me."

"Oh." Elfie looked up towards a wall clock and winced. "Later than I thought. Can you serve yourselves? The forks are in the crock, and there's cream in the fridge."

The neighbour and Annie ate apple pie in the kitchen.

"Elfie said you work in a music studio," she said.

"That's right. I started when I was living with my mother's cousin for a year. Her man—Uncle Robert, I called him—was related to Tezza—Tearlach on Sundays—Wilde, who owns Wildwood Studio. Aunt Mim knew I was interested in music production, so she got Uncle Rob to put in a word for me."

"It must have worked," she said.

He smiled. His eyes didn't narrow as much as Dequan's, but she was sure he was something interesting in the bloodline stakes. If Dutch and Chinese and a drop of something else produced Dequan, what sort of mix might make Elfie's gorgeous neighbour?

"I've been lucky," he said.

Annie ate a forkful of pie. It was very good, so she followed it up with another. Then she said, "Matt...that *is* your name?"

"Matin. Matt's fine. Just not Matty, please."

"Okay. Matt, I'm being cheeky, so don't answer if you'd rather not."

"That sounds ominous."

"No. I'm just intrigued. You look a bit, or rather a lot, like someone I know, so I was wondering where you were born."

His head moved back in a shying motion.

"Ignore that, then," she said hurriedly. "I have some Russian ancestry—a great-great-grandmother—mixed in with Irish. It doesn't show in me, but my cousin looks a bit foreign. My grandmother was born in Australia, though."

"Oh, I see. I was born at a place called Skyside. You wouldn't know it." He shrugged. "I've lived in or around Sydney since two-thousand-and-eight."

"Family?" she ventured.

"Parents, a married sister, and a younger brother. You?"

"Parents and one cousin, Olla. No siblings."

He scraped his bowl clean, got up unhurriedly, and rinsed it. "I need to go. Tez will be doing his nut. Can you tell Tam I'll call round tomorrow?"

"To check on the plumbing?"

He laughed. "I hope I subdued the leak, but you never know with leaks."

"You never do."

Annie ate her last piece of pie and licked the fork. "Yum. See you around, Matt."

"Probably," he said.

He hesitated, then walked out of the kitchen. A couple of minutes later, Annie saw him striding past the garden gate, presumably heading home to collect his vehicle.

I could have offered him a lift.

Idiot. You're not ready to go, and how would he get back?

I'll see him again... probably. He didn't say he hoped so.

Sighing, she picked up the remaining bowl of pie and took it into the other room where Elfie was still focused on her work. She put down the bowl, well clear of the papers, and flexed her shoulders.

"Sit down, do," Elfie murmured.

Annie sat. A sheaf of brochures caught her attention and she leaned over to draw them closer.

Concerts.

She ruffled through them, seeing names she knew and some she didn't.

Counterpoint, Oakengrove, Macquarie Bay, Party in the Park, Winterwatch...

Winterwatch.

She was back there with Dequan. She been twitchy from sitting and had gone for a run, then later he'd climbed Dancing Tor with her. It had been so lovely.

He skipped out on several sets to climb with you. Explain to me again—how was that not enough commitment for you?

Elfie flipped her pencil across the table and leaned back, putting her hands behind her head in a stretch.

She held the pose for a moment, then apparently spotted the pie, which she pulled closer and began to eat.

She glanced at Annie. "Sorry about that. I go off into an art-fugue sometimes. It drives my friend, Daylight, nuts. Come up and see what you think."

Annie moved to sit across from her and swivelled the drawing block. Her lips pursed in a soundless whistle. "These are *fantabulous*," she said.

Elfie looked up with a smile. "Good. You won't want them all."

"Yes, I will," Annie said greedily. She gazed at the snaking line of figures curving across the pages. The general effect was of a crowd or a conga line, but as she focused briefly on each figure, she saw women of all ages. Some pushed prams with children or small dogs, one carried a child on her back. A white-haired woman held hands with two children. She seemed to be dancing. One very elderly woman using a stick had her face turned up to the sun. Three young women had arranged themselves into an X, a K and an I. "This is it," she said. "Everyone joining in, moving, being themselves."

Elfie blew out her cheeks. "Good. That's what I was aiming for. What do you want to call it?"

"Move-a-Licious," Annie said.

"Okay. We can work that into a poster. Are you using the same logo?"

"I think so. It's a brand."

Elfie finished her pie and looked about. "Where's Matin?"

"He sorted the plumbing. He says he'll see you tomorrow," Annie said.

Elfie nodded. "Did he get his pie?"

"Yes. We ate in the kitchen."

"Okay." Elfie pushed her bowl away. "Let's break this up a bit…"

Chapter Five: Tightrope

MOVE-A-LICIOUS PROVED popular, though it was somewhat chaotic before it found its balance. Annie chose to hold it on Mondays, for the sake of alliteration.

For the first session, she borrowed Debussy. The spaniel was a calm and dignified dog, and Annie thought her presence would help Annie herself remember to keep the emphasis on health and fun. She was unlikely to find herself jogging on the spot or turning cartwheels if she had Debussy in hand.

She was right.

Reverie Eden agreed placidly that Debussy might sometimes go to the Fairy Gardens with Annie... "As long as she enjoys it."

Annie caught the oblique warning. "If she seems bored or irritated, I'll let her rest in the chapel, and that will be the last session for her."

"Thank you," Reverie said. "She's a rescue, but I think she probably had a good home once—most likely her owner passed on or became ill and somehow no one made provision for Debussy." She caught Annie's eye and said dryly, "That will never happen to her again. If anything untoward happens to me, Didymus will care for her, or, failing that, she will go to our son or to Jodiel and Foster."

"Your son?"

"Yes, Hymnal. He's wandering around somewhere in the star pin, we think. He'll be home when he's ready."

Annie reflected that it was probably time she went home for a visit. She'd been so busy she'd barely given a thought to her family, except when Matin asked about them. She frowned a little. He'd rather sidestepped her admittedly impertinent question about his antecedents. Well, he had every right to.

She thought about him sometimes. She'd decided he and Elfie were probably together, but then, he hadn't lingered after sorting out her plumbing.

Maybe they were neighbours with benefits.

Annie surprised herself with a quick flash of distaste...or something. Wariness? After some thought, she identified it as a feeling that getting romantic with a neighbour was probably not sensible. After her break with Dequan, she'd been able to avoid him easily enough by staying away from 22 Abigail Street, but what if she or her parents had lived at Number 24? Or even Number 19? It would have been uncomfortable.

None of your business, she told herself.

The only business she had with Elfie was *business*. She'd better forget about trying to make friends with such a reticent person, especially one with a tasty neighbour. It should be easy enough to stay clear of two people who lived an hour or so up the coast. After all, she hadn't encountered Dequan since their breakup, and *he* lived no more than two suburbs away from her eggbox studio.

A week later, Annie was standing in the foyer of one of the tall old buildings in the light industrial region. She'd been to a climbing shop—Pitons on Ice—where she'd invested in some high-tensile rope.

She didn't expect to get her Blondin and Barnum sessions moving anytime soon, but there could be no harm in a bit of practice.

No, a *lot* of practice, she thought. If she were going to teach clients some advanced and eclectic athletic skills, she would need to brush up on her own.

If I can even still do it.

She blinked. She'd learned to walk a tightrope on a holiday up north when she was nine. She couldn't remember exactly how that had come about—wait—it was when Grandad Pete and Granny went to Granny's school reunion. Granny Katie had spent a few days with old classmates, reacquainting herself with crocodiles, termite mounds, mud crabs, mangroves, and other mysterious Territory matters, while Grandad and Anastasia found themselves in the midst of a scout camp near the river, where a man in a short-sleeved khaki uniform was demonstrating rope-walking.

Darwin 2005

Anastasia watched as boys and girls dressed in mini-versions of the uniform stepped confidently onto the knee-high rope braced between two stalwart trees, took one, two, or three steps, and promptly fell off onto thoughtfully-placed rubber pads.

When Grandad shook his head over it all and started to move on, Anastasia grasped his arm and begged to stay.

"I could do that."

He didn't deny it. He just said, "You're not a scout, so I don't think..."

"No, but I could do it." She flipped over to walk on her hands, something she could do easily.

A couple of the scouts took their attention from their inept and staggering fellows and watched her.

"Show-off," one said. He had dark hair and a scornful face full of freckles.

Anastasia promptly toppled over. She hadn't been showing off. Acrobatics were just things she did. They were as much a part of her as her red hair and well-rounded green eyes.

Despite Grandad's gentle reasoning that she shouldn't, she approached the instructor. "Can I have a go?"

He glanced at her. "Got a junior Blondin here, have we?"

"Yes. Maybe."

Anastasia didn't know who Blondin was. Grandad explained later that he was a famous wire walker.

The man in uniform—the scouts called him Hank—gestured to the rope. "You can have a go if your..." He hesitated, looking at Grandad.

"I'm her grandfather," Grandad said. "She can try, since it's okay with you."

Hank grinned. "I'll give you a demo." He stepped onto the rope and strolled along it before doing a kick-turn like a comedy guardsman and coming back to Anastasia. "Do you want your grandfather to help you up?"

Anastasia shook her head. "I can do it." She stepped up onto the rope and stood for a few moments, orienting herself and taking in the oddness of standing in mid-air with most of her soles unsupported. She breathed steadily, the way she did when walking on her hands.

A scout with light brown hair and an open, friendly face smiled at her and made an encouraging gesture.

Anastasia smiled back. She fixed her gaze on the second tree and stepped out. When she reached the end, she considered the kick-turn but elected to step down instead.

There was an odd silence, and Anastasia realised the scouts were all staring at her with mixed admiration and annoyance. She was, after all, a stranger and younger than they were.

Only the boy who had smiled mimed applause, mouthing something that looked like: *Wow!*

Hank whistled. "Pretty good, kid! Where did you learn?"

Anastasia said, "Just now. I've never done it before."

"You're a natural, then. Not many of them around. Want another go?"

Anastasia walked the rope again, attempted the turn, lost her balance, got back on, turned triumphantly, and returned to Grandad Petre, pink with pleasure.

She glanced at the friendly boy, who was beaming at her.

Grandad took her hand. "Come on, Grand Duchess." He sometimes called her that, on account of her name.

Anastasia flicked a wave at the scouts, and the friendly one waved back. One of his fellows gave him a shove, and he shoved back, grinning. Two of the girls made eye contact with Anastasia and shrugged, smiling. One of them swung into a handstand and toppled over.

She tried again, and the boy, with no trace of self-consciousness, caught her ankles and supported her. He shot another glance at Anastasia, but the second girl called back his attention.

"Way! Over here!"

Way? That couldn't be his name, surely.

Anastasia and Grandad walked on, not too close to the river, because, as Grandad said, there might be crocodiles.

Anastasia hoped the scouts would be still there the next day, but it was Monday, and they weren't, and neither was the rope.

She experimented at home, although it took a lot of attempts to get the rope—Grandad's tow-rope this time—taut enough. He helped her, using something he called a ratchet.

She got pretty proficient, but waiting for an adult to help set the rope up was tiresome, and Mum and Dad, though easy-going, refused to let her have it any higher than her knees.

The novelty wore off, and she hadn't tightrope-walked since she was ten.

Sydney Autumn 2019

I'll just have to practise, she told herself, hitching her bundle of rope into a more comfortable position. If I've lost the knack and can't get it back, I'll forget about it.

She went on looking up at the tickets tucked into slots flanking the lifts. According to those, the tall building housed an eclectic lot of businesses. Aside from *Pitons on Ice*, she saw *The Cool Cat Company*, *Tee-for-Three*, *Titfer's*, *Mulberry Hardware*, *Mad Uncle Trick-Shop*—and *Wildwood Studios*.

Evidently, it was on one of the upper floors.

Annie mentally edited out the apostrophe in Titfer's, supposing it referred to a hat factory. On the other hand, it might be an enterprise run by someone called Titfer. Who said the uncle was mad? Cats?

Wildwood.

She had no possible excuse to go up there, and she hadn't even known it was nearby.

But—this was where the tasty neighbour worked. It must be a fair old commute, but presumably he lived in Fiddle Bay for economy's sake.

Annie shook her head slowly at Fate's odd little ways.

She'd been staying away from Elfie and Tasty Neighbour, partly for her own self-preservation.

The lift doors clonked and opened, and a tall young man stepped out with his arms full of cable boxes.

Tasty neighbour.

But no, it wasn't. He had similar shaggy brown hair and the same odd planes to his face, but it wasn't Matin Campania. For one thing, he had no idea who she was. He stopped short to avoid running into Annie, then stumbled as someone bumped into him from behind.

"Watch it, Tezza—"

Even his voice was similar. He gestured with his chin to Annie. "Care to shift a bit?" he asked.

"Sorry." She read the name embroidered onto the pocket of his uniform shirt. "Garret." The madness of the situation must be getting to her because she added, "Were you born in Skyside?"

He gave her an odd look. "No—at Borrowdale. Why? Were you?"

"No. You look like someone I know. Two someones."

"Must be your lucky day, Gar," the other man said amiably. He added to Annie, "Can we direct you anywhere? You look a bit on the pale and loitering side."

"No, thanks. I just bought a tightrope from Piton on Ice."

"Well, I guess someone has to," the man said. He had dark hair that stuck up rather and what Annie thought of as a jockey's face, although he was too tall. And was that the hint of an Irish accent? He was middle-aged, but he looked lively.

Bet he can run.

She wondered if she should start a men's group.

No, Annie. You have enough to be getting on with.

"Take care," the possible Irishman said. It might have been meaningless, but he added, "Standing in front of the lifts is likely to get you run down by lumbering elves."

He gave the younger man a tap on the arm. "Better get those things to the van before you drop them, forget yourself, and scare the horses, Gar."

They went out through the automatic doors.

Annie followed at a safe distance.

Just how many brown-haired young men with interesting faces were there? Probably thousands.

She wondered if any of them walked on tightropes.

Men on the Move. STOP it!

Chapter Six: Spring-Heeled Annie

Winter 2019

REVISITING HER SKILLS on the rope occupied Annie's spare time for a few days, but she soon got restless. She thought about going to Winterwatch again. It had been fun, and she might catch up with Nell there.

Dequan might be there, too, so she changed her mind and started planning yet another new campaign.

Blondin and Barnum was going to have to wait until she'd brushed up on a few new skills. She'd got a unicycle and was learning to ride that, but she needed something a bit more mainstream and general.

Not Men on the Move. That was an aberration of an idea. Being in charge of her little fitness business was going to her head. She had to remember she was in this to make a living.

The trouble with having boundless energy was that her brain, like her body, liked to challenge itself. *Let's see if we can do that,* it coaxed.

She was bouncing on her toes at the dog park where she'd gone with Reverie and Debussy when it occurred to her that shoes with springs in the heels would be fun.

She researched a bit on the phone, but she found nothing like the ones she envisaged.

Nevertheless, the idea gave her a notion for the new campaign, and this time, having set aside Blondin and Men on the Move, she let it roll.

She started pondering names.

Jumping Jacks, Kickstarting, Springbok, Trampolina, Flapjacks... Most of them were already in use or else sounded silly, like puddings.

So what about Spring-Heeled Annie?

That sounded fun. It could be all about high-energy workouts run in half-hour sessions designed to get the best value out of a lunch-hour.

It would fit in nicely with Friday Fitness and Move-a-Licious—a high-kinetic program for the endlessly energetic.

She did some star jumps, high kicks, and burpees.

Maybe Jodiel would teach her some karate movements.

Heels up, knees up, backflip—firecracker! *Kites!*

A passing poodle uttered an un-dog-like squawk as Annie landed in its path.

"I'm sorry," she said to its owner.

"No harm done," the woman responded. "Seems you've got some excess energy to boil off, and this is the place to do it." She indicated a black Scottie doing zoomies and barrel rolls in the middle distance.

Annie handed her a card.

The woman perused it. "This looks like Elfie's work."

"It is," Annie said, disconcerted. She'd been disseminating the content, not the artwork. "You know her?"

"She's our club artist."

So this was another of the Dames with Dogs. Annie offered her hand. "Annie Blue."

"Jumble Sayle. And this is Franco."

Jumble—that must be a dame-name—had pink and blue hair like fairy floss and a silver teardrop appliqued on her cheekbone. She wore a wide white collar like a puritan over a kind of jumpsuit composed of diamond-shaped panels in pink and blue.

"You're an entertainer?" Annie hazarded.

"Whatever gave you that idea?" Jumble widened her very pale blue eyes, fringed with long, tangled lashes. "Don't answer that. Yes. I do acrobatic dancing." She paused a beat. "Not *that* sort. No one is ever moved to tuck a fifty in my garter, more's the pity. More like clink in my cap."

"You teach?" Annie asked with a twinge of unease.

"No. I perform. Street theatre, mostly."

"Of course. Hence the clink."

Jumble grinned at her. "Franco can walk on his front legs. I don't oblige him to—he just does it. Hup, Franco!"

The poodle sat down and scratched his ear.

"Sometimes he just does it." Jumble shrugged. "You *do* teach?" She glanced down at the card. "Obviously. I was so distracted by seeing Elfie's work I didn't actively read what it said."

Annie asked, "Did she do your business cards?"

Jumble twisted her hand and proffered a card she hadn't been holding before. "Indeed. See?"

Jumble Sayle: Illusions and Dance.

The logo showed a wheel with Jumble standing in front of it, looking wide-eyed.

"Elfie's sketching over that way if you want to catch up," the woman said, nodding to her left and palming Annie's card. "Keep mine... You never know when we might want to connect."

How very odd, Annie thought as Jumble and her poodle sauntered off. As she watched, the poodle tipped forwards, folded his hind legs neatly against his belly, and proceeded at a kind of fast trundle.

Well... Annie tipped forwards and walked on her hands for a few metres. It wasn't something she did often anymore, but it was the kind of skill anyone might lose if she stopped using it.

She *wasn't* looking for Elfie, obviously, but she found her anyway. Fortunately, she was the right way up by then.

Elfie was seated on a rug on the ground, sketching three of the dames with their dogs—a handsome Samoyed, a dalmatian, and a border collie.

She smiled at Annie. "How's Move-a-Licious going?"

"Good," Annie said. She hesitated. Maybe... "I have a new campaign in mind," she said.

Elfie didn't say, "What, another one?" She tilted her head a little. "Need some work done?"

"Yes," Annie said in a rush. "Can we meet to talk it over?"

Elfie consulted the sketch. "I can finish this in about twenty minutes. Half an hour at the rotunda?"

"Thanks." Annie smiled.

Having half an hour to kill, she ran around the dog park a couple of times, then stretched out on one of the padded seats in the rotunda and tilted her cap over her eyes.

"Hello." Elfie's voice sounded mildly amused.

Annie sat up abruptly. "Is it half an hour already?"

"Forty minutes. Sorry. I got distracted."

Elfie sat down, setting a beautifully carved wooden art case beside her. "Right—tell me about the new campaign."

Annie launched into a description of Spring-Heeled Annie.

Elfie listened for a while, then held up her hand. "May I stop you for a moment?"

"Of course!"

Elfie pushed back her wavy hair. "It's about the name. I know you're talking Spring-Heeled Annie, but Spring-Heeled Jack was a Victorian-age urban legend monster who pounced about terrifying serving maids and hurdling over roofs," she said.

Annie blinked. "Really? I didn't know that."

"Look it up," Elfie suggested.

Annie tapped her phone and found the legend, just as Elfie had said.

"That is so not the image I was looking for," she began, holding out the phone for Elfie to see the demonic figure drawn in vivid Victorian gothic form. She broke off and added, "Wow!" as she spotted the ring on Elfie's outstretched hand.

"Hm?" Elfie sounded confused.

Annie indicated her hand. "What a frabjous ring. May I see?"

Elfie extended the hand fully, turning it so the ring caught the light. It shot dazzling shards of colour like dew in the sun. It was, in every possible way, a party in a stone.

Chapter Seven: A Party in a Stone

"THAT IS SO, SO PRETTY," Annie said after a stunned couple of seconds during which envy and admiration and pure delight wrestled for supremacy. "Whatever are the stones? Aurora crystals? Mystic topaz? Surely not alexandrite?"

Elfie gave her an odd look, as if surprised.

"*Is* it alexandrite?" Annie was puzzled by how much she wanted to know. It wasn't opal, which, on account of her grandfather's find, had been her previous benchmark for beauty.

Elfie said cautiously, "It might be. I don't know much about gemstones, or even jewellery, come to that."

"I know a bit about gems," Annie volunteered.

"Oh? You don't wear any—not that I can see, anyway." Elfie gave her a frank once over.

Annie gave her the same explanation she'd given Dequan. She added, "Maybe I'll give my charm bracelet to my daughter, if I ever have one."

Elfie said nothing, but Annie would not let herself fall into despondency. She smiled brightly. "I read up on gemstones when I was living with my ex. I wanted to have an informed opinion when—I thought it was when—he popped the question. He had...has...an interesting collection of curios. His granny has a habit of giving him odd things on his birthdays and at Christmas."

Okay, she was babbling now, and not kindly.

She really liked Elfie, or Tamzin, or T or whatever her first name really was. She wished her joy and happiness and success and everything good...but... There was the *but*. Why had she not let Dequan know she was okay? Why would she leave him overnight and never be back in touch?

You broke him.

The thought was ridiculous, melodramatic, and highly unfair. How could she blame a probably frightened teenager for doing such damage to a young man that he could never *really* focus on another woman?

Dequan was so very far from being a pitiable broken man, but there was *some* barrier he put up, consciously or not, that kept people he should love on the other side of a translucent wall. Maybe that was on him—*probably* that was on him...but just a note, a call, from his girl would have saved months, if not years, of anxiety.

You might have taken away my chance of that daughter...a lovely tousle-headed little girl with my flexibility and his distinctive looks.

That was unfair, and Annie was ashamed of herself—and a little ashamed of Dequan that he should let a mystery from nearly a decade ago influence him today.

She could fix it right now if she chose. Not for me—that chance is past—but for his new girlfriend.

There was a new girlfriend, she knew. Jezz had mentioned her during their most recent *Wasserplatte* get-together.

"She's tall and elegant...sort of like a saluki," Jezz had said. "Fair."

"Like you?" Annie recalled her almost-made observation about Dequan's chocolate-box-assortment of flavours in girlfriends.

"Nothing like me. She's one of those Nordie types—Dutch, like his mum." Jezz ate a slice of lemon without so much as a grimace. "Her name's Puck."

"Puck. As in *where the bee sucks, there suck I*?"

"Apparently. It's used as a girl's name in the Netherlands."

"I see. Well—"

"Yes, *well*," Jezz said. "We can both wish them luck, I guess—at least for the next two or so years until she jumps ship."

"I do wish them luck. I really do."

She really did.

"Maybe she'll..." she ventured.

"Settle? Not her. She's upmarket. He's batting out of his league with that one."

Jezz so rarely made unkind comments that Annie's brain stumbled.

Jezz ate another piece of lemon.

"Sorry. That was uncalled for."

Annie closed her eyes for a couple of seconds against that bitter little memory and summoned her usual equable self.

She wondered if Elfie could be termed upmarket but no—Elfie was uncategorisable.

"Anyway, I read up on the properties of gemstones," she said. "I like the party-in-a-stone gems best—opals, ammolite—not that anyone could afford those—but I do love colour. Unfortunately, most of the party stones are either unsuitable for constant wear, too expensive, or synthetic."

She was babbling again, but at least she'd got off the subject of Dequan.

The ring flashed as Elfie clasped her hands.

Annie put down the phone and said in a rush, "I'm going to be horribly nosy and ask where you got that gorgeous piece."

Elfie shied back, almost the same way Matt had when she asked about his birthplace.

"I'd love to know. It's so exactly what I was daydreaming of when getting engaged seemed a probability. This is a dress ring, of course, but all the better. Why shouldn't I treat myself to a gorgeous ring? That way, if I ever do get engaged, and if the man chooses an emerald or a cubic zirconia or a chunk of topaz he mined in India or whatever, I can love it for his sake, while still having exactly what I want already on my other hand."

94

She half reached out to touch the ring, then drew her hand back as Elfie said, in almost an apology, "It's not costume jewellery. It's a betrothal ring. Like an engagement ring but worn on the other hand."

Annie felt sheepish. "I just assumed it was a dress ring. Being on your right hand and all." She added, "I see now it's not something you'd buy for yourself."

"There's nothing to stop you from getting something just as lovely," Elfie said in an encouraging voice. "This ring is a commissioned piece. I don't think there are others just like it, but some jewellers let you design your own."

"Did you do that?"

"No. I left it in Aureate's hands. She's the jeweller."

"It's *gorgeous,* whatever the stones are. And I doubt if that's rolled gold." She held up her hand and dragged the elephant into the room. "I'm assuming the lucky man is your yummy neighbour?"

"Yes," Elfie said quietly. "Although I'm afraid you were a bit misled. He's not exactly a neighbour. He lives not far from the studio where he works. That's—"

"Near Piton on Ice," Annie said. "I noticed the Wildwood name on the directory when I was buying rope."

"That's it." Elfie turned the ring thoughtfully on her hand, not ostentatiously, but avoiding meeting Annie's gaze. "I don't know if you remember, but back when we first met, you told me not to take him for granted. That was a kind of breakthrough for me. I realised I couldn't bear to lose him."

Annie's uncomfortable feeling of envy and disassociation faded. Whatever had happened in Elfie's past must have been quite traumatic.

"I'm happy for both of you," she said stoutly and truthfully. "It sounds as if you know a thing or three about losing people." She held up a hand and clicked her fingers, breaking the spell. "No need to tell me anything more. I've been nosy enough, and I apologise." She looked about, making a performance of it. "Now... Where's my phone?"

"Spring-heeled Jack probably took it," Elfie said composedly, and Annie laughed.

Chapter Eight: Sparklers

September 2019 -NYE 2019

ANNIE'S NEW CAMPAIGN, renamed Sparklers, rolled out with the spring and acquired a devoted following.

There was not a lot of crossover between her campaigns, although some of the Friday Fairy Fits dipped their toes in Sparklers with varying degrees of confidence. Nevertheless, word of mouth worked for Annie. The Move-a-Licious and Friday Fit people all seemed to know someone who wanted or needed a challenge or who had resolved to get fit but could not commit to regular, long-term, or hour-long classes.

Enter Sparklers. Annie held the thirty-minute sessions three days a week, three times a day, at dawn, noon, and dusk. On the other days she offered one-on-one sessions at whatever time the client designated. It worked.

As one thirty-something woman remarked, it was difficult to come up with an excuse when a prepaid half hour awaited one. As with other sessions, the Sparklers sessions were transferable, but they could not be rolled over or rescheduled. At premium prices, the one-on-ones required a firm commitment, and it worked.

With the three campaigns running, along with one-off and occasional themed days, Annie was busier than she'd ever been.

Summer returned. She spent Christmas with her family and New Year's Eve with Jezz, who turned up with a friend to collect her.

Jezz was in a one-shouldered dress in her trademark dark blue, Annie had on her red one, on only its second outing, and the other woman, a curvy brunette with a heart-shaped face and a firm little chin, was dressed in white.

"We look like a flag," Annie said as she linked arms with Jezz. "Where are we going?"

"Up to the Fairy Gardens," Jezz said. "There's a free concert and dancing."

The other woman said she hoped for karaoke.

Annie hoped not for it, but she smiled anyway. She leaned round Jezz as they reached the car. "You look a bit familiar, but I don't think we've met," she said to the brunette.

Jezz unlocked the doors with a click and a flash of lights. "Anastasia Blugle—Delphine DiConti. You might say we three share an intimate acquaintance."

"Oh," Annie said. She blurted, "What did you do with the Shakespearean *wunderkind*?"

Delphine insinuated herself in the car with the air of a film star, or perhaps a Siamese cat. "Darling, I married him."

"That was quick." Jezz sounded amused. "Hop in the back, Annie. I've got a dressing case in front."

"Only temporarily," Delphine assured them. "For a wedding chapel commercial." She rolled her large, expressive eyes as Annie got in beside her. "He then eloped with the sound man, and I threw my shoe at him. It missed his nose by this much—" She held up two fingers. "Only it hit the busby mic and—*Goodnight New York.*"

"Did you still get paid?" Jezz asked, clicking on her seatbelt.

"I did," Delphine said. "With a loading for my pain and suffering. I gave them a rendition of Woman Scorned. The clip went viral." She sighed deeply. "After that, I had another little walk out with Dequan..."

"What?" Jezz sounded sharp.

"I know, I know...but you know how it is..." She looked up at Annie with something like apology. "You'd left him, and I was on my own, and we commiserated with one another, but you can't warm up cold pasta.

It goes all gluey and lumpy. We said goodbye again..." She patted the seat beside her. "So that's me all 'fessed up. In you get."

Annie got in.

There *was* karaoke at the Fairy Gardens. There was also an impressive line-up of bands, all lit by twinkling fairy lights strung through the trees and by lanterns.

Most of the bands were playing unplugged in a natural amphitheatre.

It was a while since Annie had been dancing, except during the Move-a-Licious sessions, and she made the most of it. People took off their shoes and piled them in a makeshift mountain at one side of the grassy stage, apparently trusting to luck and morality that they would be able to find them later.

The Fairy Gardens, a little like Hush Park, had an interesting *air* to it, Annie thought. Maybe it was the lack of vehicles, but she could not imagine anyone committing evil acts in there. It just felt—safe.

"This is the shoe I threw at Oberon," Delphine confided, holding up a slender white stiletto before tossing it onto the pile after its fellow.

Annie stared at it. "You might put an eye out with that."

"Not with Del's aim," Jezz said placidly.

"She hit the busby mic."

"Ah, but I was aiming for Oberon's long nose," Delphine said.

It was a somewhat surreal evening, but Annie enjoyed it. She tried, and mostly succeeded, not to think about the last New Year's Eve, when Foster Drake's unexpected illness had wrecked her plans with Dequan.

She wondered if Jodiel and Foster were holding the floating party this year. They'd postponed it last year, but as far as she knew, they'd never actually rescheduled.

Maybe a New Year's party just didn't work if held at some point in January when the host felt able to face a glass of bubbly.

Then, on New Year's Day, she'd tried to arrange the replacement celebration of a date night at the movies.

And how did that work out for you?

Del had got hold of a mic which must be plugged into a genny or a battery. She was belting out "Dance Me" with a good deal of drama.

The applause turned to yells of *Encore,* so Del hit them with "Fairy Tale."

Jezz muttered, "She's missed her vocation... Ought to be on stage."

"Isn't she?"

"Oh...right."

Del was just storming down the last chorus when her voice cracked. She gasped and recovered for a strong finish, then passed the mic to the MC, who demanded to know if everyone was having a good time.

Del came back to Annie and Jezz swinging her hips.

"What happened?" Jezz asked.

Del necked a bottle of something that gleamed wickedly in the lights. She swallowed half the contents, spluttered, and said, "I saw *them.*"

"Who? Oberon and the sound guy?"

"No! Dequan and his Dutch treat. Get me out of here!"

Annie said, "It's just a few minutes until midnight."

"She's right. Don't let our joint ex ruin the moment. After all, he didn't do any of us *wrong.*" Jezz gave it a definite American twang. Maybe Del wasn't the only performer among them.

Annie giggled, surprising herself. "Let's see the old year out, at least."

"We can make it a tradition," Del said. "The Three Flees."

"I *beg* your pardon?"

"F-L-E-E-S," Del said. "And in a year or so, we shall be the Quad Squad."

"You're going to invite Puck?" Jezz said.

"Why not? We're all friends. Why would we not extend our hands...if not our shoes...to a new member of Dequan's Discards?"

Or we could invite Elfie and become Five Alive, Annie thought. But that was going *too* far.

"Two minutes!" yelled the compare.

"Quick!" Annie said. "What do we want for twenty-twenty?"

"I want to learn to walk the tightrope!" Del said.

"What—why?" Jezz sounded disconcerted.

"There's a new film in the wind, a biopic of Vittoria Bellini, set in an Italian circus at the turn of the twentieth century. My agent told me about it, and I said I could do basic acrobatics." She shrugged. "I can—but turns out *my* basic is not *her* basic. I can either back down or get up to standard. You, Anastasia?"

"I'll *teach* you to walk the tightrope in my brand new Blondin and Barnum class."

"Yay!" Del, who seemed thoroughly above herself, turned to Jezz. "You, Jezabel?"

"I will design costumes for you and Annie to wear *when* you learn to walk the tightrope."

"And I'll get in touch with Jumble Sayle," Annie said.

The other two stared at her.

"Just someone I know. Her dog can walk on his front legs."

"Er—"

"Sorry. No idea what I meant there."

"Ten, nine," began the compere.

"Eight, seven," chimed in the dancers.

"Six, five, four, three—"

"That's us!" Del said.

"Two, one—"

Happy New Year!

One of the musicians played a rattle on his kettle drum, and a dark-haired alto in a mediaeval gown began singing "Auld Lang Syne" a cappella.

A pleasurable chill ran down Annie's back.

Old acquaintances would never be forgotten, but for now, she was open to some new ones.

Part Three: Plus One
Chapter One: The Casting Catalogue

February 2020

DESPITE ANNIE'S INITIAL confidence, teaching Delphine DiConti to walk a tightrope proved beyond her—at least, in the time they had available.

None of the other five women in the class learned to do it either. When, after the first session, it became clear no one had any aptitude for the activity, Annie suggested to Delphine that she might spread the word among others in the theatre world.

Delphine looked at her in astonishment. "Why would I?"

Annie said, "Word of mouth is how I get most of my clientele."

"I suppose I see that, but—"

Jezz, who had joined them to see how her prototype rope-walking designs fared in the field, gave Annie a reproving look. "Hold on, Annie. Think about why Del wants to learn rope-walking."

"For a role," Annie said. "Oh."

"Oh," Jezz echoed. "Actors are a competitive lot. So are designers, I suppose. Do you think I hand Qin-Find's details to my peers and rivals? I do not. He's perfectly at liberty to source vintage cloth for anyone, but I'm not about to offer him up to my competition on a plate."

"I suppose not. So Del doesn't want her rivals learning the skills she's learning."

"Same deal," Del said. "If they find you independently, all's fair and equal, but I'm not sharing my contacts on purpose. Why would I lessen my own chances?"

Why would she indeed? Annie reflected that there were probably far more early-career actors than there were roles for them to fill.

"And before you pile in on me, no one else I know would do it either. I would never sabotage anyone, obviously, and if someone made a misstep in a chorus line I'd grab her before she face-planted. If someone came in tipsy, I *might* suggest it was a tummy bug. If—"

"I get the picture," Annie said, laughing. She recalled her own relief that Jumble Sayle, whose skills were similar to hers, didn't want to teach.

After five lessons, none of the students had made it to the end of the rope...

Del didn't get a call out for the role in the biopic. She was surprisingly philosophical about that. "The girl who got cast used to do Summer Circus every year, so she can do all her own stunts," she explained to Annie and Jezz at the end of the first cycle of Blondin and Barnum.

"Sorry about that." Annie felt something of a failure. Most of her students succeeded in their goals. Evidently, tightrope walking was more challenging to teach, or maybe to learn, than her other campaigns.

As one of her students, having hit the rubber padding for the fifteenth time, put it, "You make it look so easy."

And maybe that was the problem. For Annie it *was* easy.

"It was worth a try," Del said. "And now I know not to put *advanced* acrobatics on my resume." She chuckled.

"What's funny?" Jezz demanded. They were sharing another *Wasserplatte*. The semi-regular get-together at Der Kaffeetanz now included Delphine as a matter of course. Puck hadn't joined them. She was still with Dequan.

Delphine said, "There's one old school actor who reputedly claimed to have *any* skill *any* role demanded. Having bluffed his way into roles he'd get up to speed before shooting started. That was back in the day. You wouldn't get away with it now."

Annie thought of the constant stream of information and gossip about celebrities. "I suppose not. You'd have any number of old friends and enemies ready to blow your cover if you claimed you could fly a plane or tame a lion when you couldn't."

"Way too many official records," Del said. "Since the Casting Catalogue came online, they can afford to pick and choose."

"The what?" Annie asked. Someone had to.

"The Casting Catalogue." Del gave it capital letters. "It's a database of actors and crew, singers, doubles, extras, and what-have-you."

"Like an agent's list?" Jezz asked. "They've been around forever, surely."

"The Casting Catalogue is way broader than that. The way it works is like this: just about everyone can edit the files—like a wiki—but it's opt-in/opt-out. For example, I could opt out of being included."

"Have you?" Jezz sounded amused.

"No. It would be professional suicide. You can also get blackballed for life if you claim a skill or experience and can't deliver, which is why I had a shot at learning to walk the tightrope rather than claiming I could and hoping to learn in time."

Jezz nodded understanding. "I see what you mean. I'd soon lose traction if I put myself forward as a designer of high-end evening wear."

Del went on, "The actors' side of the database is searchable but—get this—not by name or by role. The search terms are all quite specific. Just say there's a role for a forty-something freckle-faced ginger who can sing opera. The casting director...or a minion...would plug in search terms. Male, redhead, freckles, tenor...they might add an age range, say, forty-five plus-or-minus five years. They might put in height or body type if it mattered. Generally, the fewer search terms you put in, the bigger pool of prospects you get, but each extra term helps zero in on what you want. Once you get down to five names or so, you can start fine-tuning by personality, eye colour, and so on."

"That sounds clinical," Jezz said.

"It is, but the beauty of it is that the algorithm pays no attention to fame.

"Let's say you put in your terms... Tall, brown-haired, aristocratic-looking, able to ride a horse, forty-plus-or-minus-five-years. One of the names that came up would be Gerhard De Graff. He matches the terms exactly. Okay, but, say he's committed to a long-running drama series, and you have to shoot in the next six months. That washes him out, but there could be four or five other names giving you actors of the same general body type and colouring with a similar skill set. There might be a variance in age of five or ten years. One might be well-known, and two might be rising stars and two practically unknown, but you might be able to trade off star-power for costings and availability and so on." She wafted her hand. "What you *wouldn't* get would be prospects like...say...Gee-Jay Dare. He's in the right age demographic. He's got the brown hair, and he can ride—remember him as the sleazy trooper in *Transportation*? He wouldn't come up though—he's not aristocratic-looking. He can do flash or sleazy or grimy, but not blue-blood."

"Doesn't this reinforce typecasting?" Jezz asked.

"I expect so, but there are still some roles with no pre-set appearances tagged." Del shrugged. "You could just say, *Banjo player, male* if you wanted."

Annie asked, "Have you ever put yourself into the search?"

"Of course," Del said. "We all do it." She crunched into a gherkin and raised her brows as she watched Jezz consume a jalapeno. "Anyone who says she doesn't is probably lying." She sighed. "At one point, there was a rumour that the more targeted searches you made the more likely your name was to come up for other people's searches, but that's not so. It's been proved that if a new name enters the database and happens to match the parameters then he—or she—is every bit as likely to turn up in a search as any A-lister. It might reinforce typecasting, but it also gets unknowns or lesser-knowns to the consideration stage."

"Casting by numbers," Jezz said.

"Sort of. But it saves everyone wasting time with the unsuitable and unavailable. For example, if the target is a nineteen-year-old brunette who can roller-skate, the algorithm won't offer a thirty-year-old blonde who can't. It may serve up a seventeen-year-old or someone who's twenty-two or three, but she *will* be brunette, or at least willing to become so, and she *will* be able to roller-skate. Remember, if she claims she can and it can be proved she can't, she's dropped from the database."

"That sounds almost too practical," Annie said. "What happens if you put in a..." She paused.

"An impossible combination, such as a woman two metres tall with heterochromia and limbo dancing skills?" Jezz inserted.

"It will invite you to widen the parameters. It *won't* give you someone who is one point seven metres with green eyes and jazz ballet skills...unless, of course, you specifically instruct it to find *the closest available match*. In that case, it would probably give you the tallest available woman in the age range, on the grounds that she could wear contact lenses and *learn* limbo dancing.

"If you don't specify *closest available match* then it won't waste your time if it can't give you what you asked for." She shrugged. "Now I can add a couple more skills to my entry, thanks to you, Annie. I didn't make the grade as a rope-walker, but *damn,* did I master the unicycle and the cartwheel."

Annie smiled abstractedly. An idea had struck her, and she was unsure what, if anything, she should do with it.

Chapter Two: Jogging on the Spot

Sydney March 2020

ANNIE CONTINUED TO enjoy her catch-ups with Jezz and Del, but by the autumn, she'd started to feel a familiar restlessness, and that made her feel both ungrateful and a bit guilty.

Despite the relative failure of Blondin and Barnum, her fitness campaigns were doing well. Nevertheless, she felt somewhat detached from life, as if she were jogging on the spot and going nowhere.

Her times with Jezz and Del were fun, and she sometimes spent time with Jodiel Drake, but it was all starting to feel routine. Eating at Der Kaffeetanz or window shopping in the city or even sailing on the harbour with the Drakes were all enjoyable up to a point, but Annie was increasingly aware that these activities were more to the taste of the others than to hers. Jezz enjoyed trawling for inspiration in op shops and antique emporiums, Del looked at clothing from an acting point of view, and Jodiel's life revolved around her husband and her martial arts.

What's in it for me? That was a churlish attitude, but what *was* there for Anastasia Blugle in the life of Annie Blue?

"The problem is I'm making a living from what used to be my favourite activity," she told Reverie Eden one day.

Reverie had come to fetch Debussy, who had an appointment with the vet and who had, oddly if understandably, gone to ground under Annie's bed.

"Very strange," as Reverie said. "It's just a yearly check-up. She's not going to be hurt or frightened, and I have no idea how she even knew it was happening today." She dropped a treat near the edge of the bedspread, and they waited to see if Debussy would emerge.

One could not, as Reverie pointed out, burrow under the bed and haul out such a dignified dog.

"I see your point about routines," she added, after a short pause. "Running and exercise have always been your way of letting off steam. Now your subconscious looks at it as work, so your steam valve is clogged."

Annie huffed a laugh. "Nice analogy. How about you? Do you find being a minister has taken away any of your enjoyment of...er..."

"Offering guidance and help when I can?" Reverie suggested.

"More or less."

"No. But then, I was ordained comparatively late in life. I can carry out such ministry as I'm inclined while socialising at the dog park or enjoying conversations and study with interested and interesting people."

Debussy's snout edged into view, took the treat, and retracted again.

Reverie laid down another treat a little closer to the door.

"If it ever started to feel routine or ministry by numbers, I would retire or take a sabbatical," she added. "I have the luxury of doing that, because Didymus is working and I'm not in charge of a parish. I would need to attend to any weddings or baptisms I had scheduled, but I could clear my calendar by not booking any others."

"I feel silly and ungrateful," Annie admitted. "I've achieved my goal, and it's working better than I ever hoped, but somehow—"

"If you go for a run around the Fairy Gardens it probably feels like work rather than recreation."

"That's it exactly."

"Maybe you might look at some other activity as recreation," Reverie suggested as Debussy edged back into view. "What else have you enjoyed doing?"

Annie gave it some thought. "I used to like metal detecting with Grandad. It was exciting when he found a gorgeous opal ring. But

I don't feel like doing that by myself. The chances of interesting discoveries are too low to be worth the effort." The memory of that ring reminded her of something else. "One of the *best* days I ever had was with my ex at a music festival, one called Winterwatch."

"So you enjoy live music?"

"Not really. I like dancing, but just sitting listening isn't my idea of fun. I'm more of a doer than a spectator."

"Why was this particular day so memorable?" Reverie prompted.

"We climbed Dancing Tor. It was...fantabulous. Dequan went to the festival for the music, but he voluntarily gave up one afternoon to climb with me. He enjoyed it, too. It was a *top of the world* day."

"Perhaps climbing is what you crave." Reverie put down two more treats. "It's physical exercise but different from running or acrobatics or martial arts, or dancing, come to that. It's a challenge, and you get rewarded with a view."

"There's nothing to stop me from going climbing, but it's a bit like sailing—not clever to do it alone. And none of my friends are climbers, as far as I know." She couldn't imagine Jezz or Del scrambling up a mountain.

"Jodiel certainly isn't," Reverie said. "She can break a brick with her hand, but she's not too fond of heights. There's sailing, but I suppose you'd have to be a crew member to enjoy that."

Debussy emerged until half of her was visible, and Reverie dropped a gentle hand on the spaniel's ruff. "Come on, my dear. Time to go. Doctor Belle will be pleased with you, I'm sure."

Debussy rolled her eyes around to look at Annie, who held up both hands, distancing herself.

The spaniel sighed.

Reverie clipped on a leash Annie hadn't realised she had. As she led the resigned dog out of the eggbox studio, she glanced over her shoulder at Annie. "Maybe you're really looking for a companion who enjoys the same things you do. Compromise is all very well, but you shouldn't need to do it all the time."

"No," Annie said. She added, "It's finding someone that's the problem."

"Make a list," Reverie advised. "Write down a selection of attributes, the *must haves,* the *it would be nice* things, the *sticking points,* and the *optimum but not essentials.*"

"Thanks. Maybe I will."

"It worked for me," Reverie said.

Annie watched her landlady and her frequent visitor departing.

Have I just been ministered to, or was that a simple conversation?

She lifted a shoulder in a partial shrug. It didn't seem to matter. Reverie was a kindly presence without being sweet or smarmy... She'd allowed Debussy to keep her dignity intact.

She's never in a hurry.

I always am.

She had her phone and half an hour before she needed to set out for the next Move-a-Licious session.

But—typing on a phone was awkward.

Annie went to fetch a pen and paper.

Chapter Three: Where it Listeth

March 2020

ANNIE SAT AT HER MINUSCULE table with a sheet of scrap paper.

She pondered her first move, put aside the paper, and fetched a pretty notebook Granny Katie had given her when she was twelve. It had never been used because Anastasia had never been a contemplative person.

Perhaps that was part of what was missing from her life.

Annie deliberately spent time admiring the little book.

Granny, she realised belatedly, had known what she was doing. The notebook, instead of presenting puppies, kittens, butterflies, unicorns, mermaids, or whatever had been popular with preteens in the first decade of the 2000s, featured a riot of colours in an abstract design that implied, *I'll still be here when you catch up with me.*

It might be a flurry of birds or a huge Escher posy of exotic flowers, but it might equally be something else.

The colours, Annie saw, celebrated opal and alexandrite, peacocks and bornite, lustre ware and mother of pearl, abalone shell, and all the loveliness she'd seen encapsulated in Elfie's betrothal ring.

A party in a stone.

Annie opened the cover and wrote down some things she'd hardly let herself think of, let alone expressed.

The wind bloweth where it listeth.

Okay, that wasn't quite the same as making a list, but it worked.

Freedom.

I'm self-employed. I live an autonomous life. I do what I enjoy doing, and I make a reasonable living doing it.

She paused, then added honestly, *That's partly because my landlady charges me a ridiculously small rent on account of me not giving her any trouble.*

I have a visiting dog, without the responsibility for a pet. That's also on account of my landlady.

My students like me, and I like them. They pay me for a service that is of benefit to them as well as to my coffers. My system holds them accountable, and they appreciate that.

I have friends I can call if I want to go out in company. They understand the boundaries of my occupation, and they'll break up the party early or reschedule and not hold it against me.

Jezz and Del are single, so I don't feel like a third wheel.

Jodiel is casual and not joined at the hip with her husband.

Elfie...

She paused again, for longer this time, aware that Elfie wasn't available for going out on the town. Elfie wasn't a friend. She just felt like someone who ought to be one.

Elfie has what I want.

There.

She skated over that, because envy wasn't an admirable quality.

Lucy...spends half the year on an island and is fiercely loyal to Dequan.

That was another thing. Four of the five women she thought of as friends were closely connected with Dequan, who had so nearly been the companion she wanted.

So why didn't you hang in there? Or have another try? Del did.

And see where that got her.

It's complicated.

Annie's phone beeped.

Time to go.

Work called, but she almost wanted to stay in her cosy eggbox studio, hiding out from the world and communing with her notebook.

Nonsense.

Annie slid the notebook and pen into the little drawer under the table, laced on her running shoes, grabbed her prepacked bag, and headed out.

Chapter Four: Must-Haves and Maybes

March 2020

FOR ALMOST THE FIRST time, Annie found herself impatient with her multiple Move-a-Licious sessions. She had the habit of focus, but there was an itch in the back of her mind all the same. After the evening session, she was glad to farewell the last of her lingering students and walk back through the Fairy Gardens. Usually, she ran.

Maybe it was time to bring Debussy to another session. The company of a contemplative dog was a good remedy for too much haste in the brain.

She noted the shadows lengthening. Soon the clocks would change, and she'd have to consider her schedule. The Fairy Gardens almost made the perfect venue, but she might have to drop the first and last sessions or change the times. No, that wouldn't work. Some of her students came in early and needed time to go home and shower before work, and those who came after work or after the school pick-up would be unable to come earlier.

I might have to shift to more one-on-ones for winter, she thought, but the idea didn't appeal. Group dynamics played a large part in the success of her campaigns. The Move-a-Licious participants treated their sessions as a social occasion without the coffee and cake—in theory, that was. Apparently some of them convened at one of the local cafes afterwards.

Annie drove home, passing Belmore Park. The floodlights were on, though it was still daylight. Maybe she could relocate the first and last sessions there.

She wondered if she'd need a permit such as the one she had for the Fairy Gardens. She'd signed an agreement with one of the Dames with Dogs—Caddy Hildebrand—a representative of the le Fay family, who had endowed the gardens. This allowed her to hold exercise classes there as long as she and her students did no damage and didn't impede on others' enjoyment of the gardens. It was a straight-forward and reasonable requirement, typical of the Dames. Sometimes, Annie wished fervently that the Dames with Dogs might administer the local government.

Possibly whoever managed Belmore Park would have a similar agreement, though it was probably too much to hope for a Dame to represent them.

Annie was still pondering this when she reached home. Debussy was waiting for her.

"Not too traumatised by the vet, then?" Annie asked, smoothing the spaniel's ears.

Debussy gave her a friendly nudge.

"You can come in, but no disappearing under my bed. There are probably dust bunnies, and they can't be good for you."

While the dog settled on a convenient carpet square, Annie showered and assembled a meal of chicken, capsicum, and pasta, which she ate with a crumble of feta and a grinding of black pepper while rereading her notes.

"All very well as far as it goes," she remarked to Debussy, "but it's about the life I have now, not about what I want for the future. It just clarifies why the companions I have currently aren't right for this purpose."

She pushed aside her plate, gave a piece of reserved chicken to her guest, and picked up her pen again.

What had Reverie suggested?

Write down a selection of attributes, the must haves, *the* it would be nice *things, the* sticking points *and the* optimum but not essentials.

So she was looking for a companion to share her free time—someone to join her in active pursuits that differed from things she did for work—someone for whom she need not make physical allowances. Or at least, not too many.

Active, she wrote. That was a *must have*—someone who would be happy to move quickly and with purpose rather than wander along looking in shop windows or observing passers-by.

Not that there was anything wrong with that, she thought fairly, and for Jezz and Del and even Elfie, it was probably a job requirement, but it needed something to balance it. She supposed any fit person *could* drop to a saunter, but the natural saunterers probably could *not* freeclimb a cliff.

Someone with a life, she wrote. *Someone who already has active interests but no close companion to share them.*

She wasn't too sure about the second bit, but it did make sense. She definitely couldn't be doing with anyone who was bored or needy.

Am I needy?

She didn't think she was, except possibly in her yearning to have Elfie as a friend.

Batting out of my league with that one. There's no Annie Blue-shaped hole in Elfie's life or in the tasty neighbour's either.

She pushed the thought away.

Well. I can be a friend to her, even if I can't have one in her. She's got him.

I couldn't bear to lose him. That's what Elfie had said.

A cold mouse of fear ran down Annie's back—not for herself, but for Elfie.

Not my business. Not my problem.

What about the deal-breakers?

No one with too much baggage. No one too competitive. No one meanspirited. No one reckless. No one unreasonable.

Am I any of those?

She was pretty sure she wasn't.

That seemed to be that.

She looked over the shortlist.

Someone who enjoys climbing or kayaking or rock-hopping or surfing or even hang gliding. Not extreme sports, but something active and interesting.

Someone who enjoys exploring and who knows lots of good places.

Someone who enjoys food but who isn't pretentious.

Someone who has a flexible schedule but who understands some people don't have that luxury.

That really had better be that. The more she put down, the fewer candidates the algorithm—

Annie's thoughts broke off with an almost audible snap. She must have stiffened, because Debussy raised her head and fixed her liquid brown gaze on Annie's face, tilting her ears with interest.

How odd that spaniels can do that!

Annie laughed shortly.

"This is all very well, but where am I going to find people like this or even look for them?" she asked the dog. "I suppose I *could* get a dog..."

Debussy snorted. She would *not* enjoy mountaineering, she implied.

Annie laughed again at the freakishly apt response then pushed the thought a bit more. If she wanted a gym bunny, she'd obviously look for one at the gym. Runners would be hanging about at races or zipping round the park at daybreak. Swimmers and surfers and kayakers would be at the pool or the beach. Climbers...halfway up mountains.

But if they've got any sense, they climb in groups or pairs, and I need someone unassigned. Third wheeling isn't what I want.

Wanted: one active, athletic, non-needy, tolerant, adventurous, affectionate, unassigned male.

It had better be a male.

One who definitely belongs to himself and not to anyone else. Aged between twenty-five and thirty-five. Healthy in mind, body, and soul.

And–might as well go all out here—*it wouldn't be a problem if he could be tall, with brown hair and a slightly unusual cast to his features. Must not have a current girlfriend and must not be bruised or obsessed with one who left him or disappeared. Must have an Annie-shaped hole in his life but, for some inscrutable reason, not have recently filled it with an ersatz Annie.*

Heavens! If she went on like this, she might as well join an online dating site and be done with it!

That was the logical solution, but, somehow, it didn't appeal.

Instead, it reminded her of an idea she'd almost had after a get-together with Jezz and Del.

Del had been describing the capital-letter-worthy Casting Catalogue, and if she remembered correctly, the onus on the listed actors was proof of any claims. Obviously, hair colour and weight might be subject to change, and an accident or illness might temporarily render someone unable to ride a racehorse, but skills and aptitudes and basic appearance had to be accurately represented. To lie, to exaggerate, or to over-or-understate was to risk excommunication.

Professional suicide.

Annie frowned. She supposed matters such as age would need to be updated regularly to force compliance.

Not if the algorithm searches by birthdate rather than age-in-years.

So the parameters might be *born between 1990 and 1996* rather than *27 years old plus-or-minus three years.*

That would work.

She sent a text to Del. Wasserplatte *this week?*

Del didn't answer immediately, but just as Annie was preparing for bed, filled with the prickle of waiting for someone else to add a link to her chain of reasoning, a response pinged back.

Jog instead? Edging out of my plus-or-minus weight zone.

Sure. When?

I can book a one-on-one any afternoon.

Surprised and amused, Annie suggested *tomorrow at two. Fairy Gardens.*

Del sent her a thumbs-up.

Chapter Five: Five DeDops

Sydney March 2020

DEL WASN'T UNFIT BY normal standards. She could dance, and, as she informed Annie, she'd had riding, fencing, and swimming lessons when she was younger.

However, she wasn't a natural runner.

"I forgot to ask how much," she remarked when they'd met at the unassuming entrance called the Founders' Gate.

"How much what?"

"Price for a session."

"Nothing," Annie said, surprised. "I invited *you*."

"You invited me for *Wasserplatte,* which we'd have gone Dutch on. I changed the parameters."

"Never mind that."

This wasn't a paid gig, but Annie did her due diligence. "Shoes comfortable?"

"Yes." Del sounded puzzled.

"Hydrated?"

"Yes. And before you ask, I'm wearing a sports bra and sunscreen. Let's go."

Annie began her warm-up. She didn't need one, but she supposed Del did. Then she ran through the breathing and pacing techniques.

Del, visibly biting her tongue, nodded intelligently.

"Officious little b," she said when Annie ran down.

"Believe it," Annie said. "You don't get to injure yourself on my watch."

She started her timer and began jogging on the spot. "Just testing your focus and lung power. Right, we'll make it an interval work-out.

Jog, walk, jog, walk. You should be able to converse normally. The moment you can't, we ease the pace."

"Yes, Mum."

They set out along the tracks that wound through ferns and flower beds.

"Why did you want to see me?" Del asked as they slowed for the final five-minute walk that would return them to the gate.

Annie hesitated, then went for it. "Can anyone search the Casting Catalogue?"

"That's the point of it," Del said, wiping her face with an Absorbo pad. "Directors search for cast prospects. Oh, and of course actors use it to scope out the competition."

"Oh?"

"Obviously, we do. Quite apart from knowing who else is in line for a role we covet, it helps us to refine our own entries. For instance, I couldn't add tightrope walking as I hoped, because I couldn't learn it, but I could add *speaks fluent Italian,* because I do. I polished it up in November when my *nonna* came for a visit. That gives me an edge on Aimee."

"Who?"

"Aimee Cummins. She routinely comes up in the same searches as I do. They might as well cast us as twins in a weekly drama and be done with it." She stretched, raising both arms above her head. "Why the interest? Thinking of registering as an extra?"

"No...well..."

"What then?" Del turned her searchlight gaze on Annie. "You could. There's always room for extras with specific skills. You could also look into training others on-set." She lit up in a dazzling grin. "Let's hie us to Der Kaffeetanz and plug you into the system. If nothing else, we can play *which big star is my doppelganger.* We can look for pseudo Annies."

"I thought we were staying away from Der Kaffeetanz."

"Not necessarily. I've earned it. I promise I'll go heavy on the *wasser* and lightly on the *platte*."

Annie opened her mouth to comment then closed it again. This wasn't a paid gig, and, besides, it was up to Del to arrange her life.

And it was up to Annie to arrange hers.

"In the broad parameters, it's amazing who we match up with," Del continued as they settled at their accustomed table at the café. She hooked a menu over with one finger. "For example, in some searches I come up alongside Dominique Fortescue. Can you believe that?"

Annie wondered if she ought to know that name.

Del went on, "We're the same height and have the same proportions, apparently, but she's decades older than I am. We both sing in the alto range, though she's an opera singer, and I'm not. We can both handle comedy, though she never does musical comedy. We have the same basic colouring until you plug in hair colour. She's embraced full-on white."

"Maybe someone will cast you as her granddaughter," Annie suggested.

"Could happen. The Catalogue works a treat for building on-screen families. It matches accents, body type, skin tone, and even facial proportions. Uncanny really...though in reality two people can score almost identical attributes but look quite different when you put them side-by-side. Aimee and I match to ninety percent, and we could pass as twins, but Tip Fettuccini, who also matches us to ninety percent...not so much."

"Oh?" Annie reflected that she'd forgotten just how much Del could talk, especially when Jezz wasn't there to balance her loquacity.

Del raised a finger to attract a server and leaned closer to Annie. "For one thing, he's a *man*."

"Fraternal twin?"

"Not possible. He doesn't walk the same way and his aura—what?"

"His *aura*?"

Del wafted her hand. "Never mind. He could *not* pass as our brother, even from another mother. He's got this weird bronze complexion, and when he forgets himself, he lapses into Gaelic."

"A man named Fettuccini speaks Gaelic."

"It's not his real name. Or maybe it is. Who knows? Lovely guy, if you like 'em small."

"Do you?"

"No. Our shared *intimate experience* is my go-to type, unfortunately." She rolled her eyes, leaned even closer, and whispered, "I've even gone hunting in the Catalogue for Dequan doppelgangers! I can hardly believe I'm admitting that to you, or to anyone."

Annie felt her eyes bug. "About that—"

"What can I get for you two?" Riva Bless had arrived, bright in her dirndl, sporting a milkmaid braid and bearing a notepad and pencil.

Just like a comedy Oktoberfester who's mislaid her stein, Annie thought distractedly.

"*Wasserplatte*," Del said. "We are *so* predictable."

"Swiss chocolate with that?"

Del sighed. "No. Black coffee."

Riva nodded and glanced at Annie.

"We'll share the platter, but no hot drink for me."

"That's right. You don't," Riva said.

"Not often, no. And could you bring an extra bottle of water?"

The server left, and Del leaned back in her chair.

For a few seconds silence reigned, and Annie tried to think of a way to nudge the conversation back on track.

Fortunately, Del continued without prompting. "I narrowed it down to five prospects."

Annie, disingenuously, mumbled a *hmm*?

"Five DeDops. All between twenty-seven and thirty-five, all guy-next-door with a touch of the exotic. One had a man bun and a beard, but I forgave that. He'd grown it for a role. Biblical epic—a spin on the Samson story from the Book of Judges."

"And?" Annie asked.

Del shrugged, then leaned back as Riva brought the *Wasserplatte.* "That was quick."

"We have an assembly line," Riva said. "Your coffee won't be long."

Annie poured herself a glass of water. "And?"

"And what?"

"Did you go out with any of them?"

Del heaved a dramatic sigh. "No—just as with names and fame and former roles, you can't put in relationship status, because it has no bearing on suitability for roles. My discoveries had all been discovered already.

"Now, let's see how *you* fare."

Chapter Six: Firecracker

Sydney March 2020

IT TREMBLED IN ANNIE'S mind to back out, but she realised in time that Del planned to put Annie herself in the system.

"What if someone tries to hire me?" she asked.

"I guess you could get hired. You could always say no. And as an extra, you don't need to be a member of Equity or have an agent or anything like that." Del bent sideways and pulled a tablet out of her bag.

"Wake up," she commanded it. The tablet blinked. "Let's hope it *takes*. The connectivity's always a bit odd in here," she added.

She tapped a few times.

"Okay, here's the Catalogue. We'd better make you a login. We *could* use mine, but it might get confused and think I'm claiming to be a natural redhead and toss me out on principle. It might also think I'm running two profiles and that's *verboten*."

She shoved the tablet in Annie's direction. "You'd better do this for yourself. You can always delete it or change it or put it on hiatus later."

Bemused, Annie oriented the screen. She briefly considered using her work email address but chose instead an old one she rarely accessed.

Oh, and do I really think the casting directors will be flocking to hire me?

"Okay, I'm in," she said. "Does it want my name?"

"No. Your name goes behind the password-protected wall. You'll be texted an identifier code."

Annie expected a string of letters and weird symbols, but instead she got a single word—*Firecracker.*

"Nice!" Del approved. "I come up as *Syringa*. I had to look it up." She nodded towards the tablet. "Before we put you in, describe someone at random and see the kinds of matches you get. Go!"

Annie blanked out. Then she remembered an odd, enigmatic film, half of which she'd caught with Grandad during a sleepover when her parents were away. Neither of them had ever been able to recall the title or the names of the tiny handful of stars. Even the main character's name eluded them, because she spent most of the film alone.

Hesitantly, she started to type.

"Female. Australian accent. Small. Born nineteen-fifty-five plus-or-minus five years. Brown hair. Ballet." It wasn't much to go on, but it scored three hits. Annie examined the three possibilities, who were tagged as Dune, Golf, and Raincloud. None was the woman she remembered, although she supposed they all fitted the demographic well enough.

Delphine peered at them and pointed to the screen. "That one at the top—Dune—is Pamela Prentiss, and the others are Dorothy Hope and Sandy Duncan Dundee. They all starred in a sit com about three school friends who met up at their forty-year reunion and found out they're all divorced. They moved in together."

Annie nodded vaguely. She hoped Del didn't intend to give her career highlights of every match that came up.

She tried again, this time describing Delphine.

"Female. Australian accent. Dark hair and eyes. Vivacious. Alto. One-hundred-sixty centimetres. Sixty kilograms. Fencing. Birthdate around nineteen-ninety-six."

Up came Delphine, along with six others.

Annie put in *speaks fluent Italian*. Three of the women dropped off the search.

"Where's the man?" she asked.

Del tapped the screen. "You specified female. Take that out and remove the Italian... There he is."

And there he was, though his hair was more dark auburn than black or brown, and his skin tone was definitely a weird shade of olive.

"That's enough," Del said. "You can go right down the rabbit hole with this one. We'll put *you* in now."

Hesitantly, Annie typed a few keywords for herself—age, ethnicity, height, weight, *short red hair, athletic, acrobatic, runner, tightrope, unicycle, roller skates.*

"That's enough," Del said. She reached over and hit *Search*. "And...zero. Zilch. *Niente*. Seems you're one of a kind. Take out the last three entries...and...*bingo!*"

To Annie's fascination, six red-headed young women flicked across the screen. Two smiled into the camera. Three looked neutral. One was caught in a flying karate kick.

"Polo, Kite, Shale, Aconite, Tiger, and Pitch. Well, well! I don't think I know any of these." Del looked them over. "But see what I mean?"

Annie saw the sisters she'd never had.

"You could definitely get a chorus line up," she said.

"If you take out *short* and leave just red hair, you'll get more matches," Del said. "You could even define it to *curly* or *updo*. Now let's create Firecracker. Put in as much detail as you want, especially in the skill set, but make sure you don't claim anything you can't back up."

Annie, diving down the rabbit hole and tumbling fast, described herself with some helpful contributions from Del.

"Don't put in subjective terms... So no *pretty, handsome, beautiful*, and definitely not *unique*," she advised. "You can use *sweet* or *solemn* or *angst*. Can you do *sweet*? I can't."

She watched Annie fill in activities. "You can walk on your hands. I've seen you. Cartwheels. Can you climb ropes?"

Annie nodded.

"Excellent. You might pick up something in that new pirate show—a very loose remake of an old movie called *Madam Sin*. You couldn't play the pirate queen, but you could be one of her crew. You haven't put dance. Can you do the splits? Or the Cossack? Yoyo tricks? Card tricks? Escapology?"

"*No*! And I don't bury myself alive, either!" Annie tried not to snap.

"Ride, row, surf, sail, skate, free-dive, parachute, sword-swallow—"

Annie was beginning to wish she'd never contacted Del, so she just shook her head emphatically. It wasn't as if she was actively looking for work as a film extra. From the little she knew about the job, it meant a lot of waiting around and possibly being yelled at, and that was something she really wouldn't enjoy.

Del may have sensed she was trying Annie's patience, because she stopped making suggestions and drank her coffee, watching Annie fumble her way through the image upload of one of the reference photos she'd had Elfie take for Sparklers.

Annie filled in her old email and her current phone number, because the screen wouldn't proceed until she did. She recorded her login details in a secret folder on her phone and logged out of the site.

Del took the tablet back and shoved it into her bag. "Right," she said briskly. "Give that a day or three to percolate into the system, then you can do a search and see if you come up. Oh, and let me know if you get any calls from agents desperate to represent you or directors who want a sexy pirate wench or an acrobatic jewel thief or a background tumbler in a fair scene..."

Annie promised willingly. She was certain she'd never hear from anyone through the site.

She and Del shared what was left of the *Wasserplatte*, split the bill, and hugged goodbye. Annie corralled the extra bottle of Fossmere, and they left in their separate cars.

Annie went home to contemplate her next move. She certainly hadn't expected her planned covert operation to look up men fitting her list to end up with Del's confession of treading the same path and somehow persuading her to register as a film extra.

But then, when did plans ever work out the way one hoped and dared to expect?

Del had a good heart. She was just—

Maybe I impress people the same way. I do come on strong when I want something.

Annie didn't forget her list and her hopes. Now she knew what she wanted, and she gave herself some time to concentrate on her life as it was. Being single offered a good many freedoms.

Chapter Seven: Webs

April 2020

FOR A FEW DAYS, ANNIE played intermittently with her profile in the Casting Catalogue. The activity had a strangely guilty appeal, inserting and removing search terms to see how it altered the results. She didn't get matched with any white-haired opera singers or with any young men, but some quite unlikely-looking people shared at least some of her attributes.

The Catalogue's fine print claimed that it didn't save searches or email login frequencies and only those with a legitimate professional reason could apply for contact details... There was a lot more, but because Annie could never work out who, if anyone, was online searching at any point, she assumed her activity was equally screened from everyone else.

So how had Del ascertained that her five DeDops were all in possession of significant others?

That was an enigma. Either Del had found some way to cheat the system or she'd done it the old-fashioned way, by finding out the identities of her targets through image matching and asking around. Obviously, Del had far more contacts in the stage and screen world than Annie and a far broader mental encyclopaedia of actors and roles.

Webs upon webs, Annie pondered. Del must have some kind of filing system in her head to keep all the layers of her life straight.

After a while, tinkering with her profile lost its appeal. Knowing she looked like an actor, code-named Pitch, who did karate was interesting, but it could not be of any practical value unless Pitch was looking for an understudy or a body double.

Annie decided that if she was going to spend time online, she should use it productively, so she rebuilt her Annie Blue website and made it more accessible.

She called Elfie to ask her permission to link to the Elf-Made Art site.

Elfie sounded pleased to hear from her, which was nice. She asked reciprocal permission to link to Annie Blue, stating that Annie's campaigns were among her favourite challenges.

That was also nice. It was on the tip of Annie's tongue to suggest...what...another meeting at the dog park? A walk along the shingle beach at Fiddle Bay? But Elfie said she and Matin were spending the weekend with his family and she needed to get ready.

"Where do they live?" Annie asked.

Elfie paused.

"Don't tell me if you'd rather not."

"It's not that—truly. It's just that you've probably never heard of the place. *I* never had."

"Try me."

"It's called Skyside. That's not a town, more of a district."

"You're right," Annie said. "I'd never heard of it until Matt mentioned it quite recently."

"Oh?"

"When we were eating pie that time...when you were working on my Move-a-Licious campaign, Matt said he was born there. I still have no clue where it is."

"Oh...well, it's a kind of shared holiday cottage—right off the grid. Matin's family gathers there sometimes to reconnect and to unwind. Not that they call it that."

"Have a lovely time," Annie said wistfully, and Elfie said she intended to.

"By the way...I never asked...Elfie's your Dame Name, I know, but I don't think you ever told me your real one."

She held her breath.

To her relief, Elfie said quite cheerfully, "My name has always been up to interpretation. Elfie *is* my Dame Name of course, but it's also my real second name. The name I use most of the time is Tamzin, though some friends call me Thomasine. It's the same name, really. You'd understand about that, though, Annie. I expect you get called a few variations, too."

"Annie, mostly, but my family still call me Anastasia or Grand Duchess, which is Grandad's little joke. My ex used to call me Stace."

"There you are then," Elfie said. "Got to go. Matin's h—" She broke off, and Annie realised Matin was indeed there, and greeting his fiancée...no, *betrothed*...with appropriate enthusiasm. It was just about six-thirty, so he must have left work early.

She ended the call before she heard something embarrassing.

After that, she went out in the yard for a vigorous ball game with Debussy and Clancy, the ebullient Irish setter belonging to Pet Donovan. Pet, whose actual name was Penthe, was not only a Dame friend of Reverie's but also one of Annie's own Friday Fitness students.

Small world.

Or was it? Maybe it was more a case of gossamer webs floating out to connect the right people with one another.

Chapter Eight: Spindle

May 2020

BY MAY, ANNIE HAD RELUCTANTLY relocated her early morning and evening programs to the quiet park. She'd been using that venue for her sessions with Bette Mallory, in any case. Bette had by now dispensed with her cane, and although she could still not do star jumps, she was faster and more certain on her feet.

When she heard that Move-a-Licious and Sparklers would be happening at the park during the late autumn and winter, she promptly dropped her one-on-one sessions and signed up for Move-a-Licious instead.

Annie was packing up after one of the evening sessions when the phone rang in her pocket, making her jump.

Belmore Park's odd acoustics had a flattening effect on music and conversation, and the phone sounded muffled, as if it had a cold.

Annie tucked a bundle of bamboo hoops under one arm, extracted the phone, and tapped the screen.

No name came up, though there was a normal-looking number, so it probably wasn't spam. She didn't recognise it, but it might be a new would-be client.

"Annie Blue," she said pleasantly.

"Good evening." The voice was male and unfamiliar. It didn't say anything more. Not a client then, unless he was calling on behalf of a wife or mother or daughter or...well, some other female relative.

"How may I help you?" Annie put down the hoops and did some plies. "Are you trying to contact someone from Move-a-Licious? The last ones left a few minutes ago."

The man said, "I'm trying to contact someone called Firecracker."

For a few seconds, Annie's mind felt blank. Then, with a rush, she remembered the Casting Catalogue.

"I'm aware this sounds peculiar," the man said. "It's not exactly a name, more of a label. It belongs to a woman with red hair who can walk on her hands and on a tightrope. Do you know of such a person?"

"That depends on what you want with...Firecracker," Annie said.

"I quite see that. It's nothing nefarious. The label came up in the Casting Catalogue search which is—"

"I know what it is. Are you a director?"

"I directed a couple of college productions at John Folly House, and I might do more, but I wouldn't style myself a *director*. It's just something I do sometimes."

"Are you an agent then? Or an actor?"

"No. And sometimes. I'm listed in the Catalogue under the label of Spindle if you want to look me up."

"You can't look up names or even labels," Annie pointed out.

"I knew that. I think. If you look up *ordinary, average, brown hair, brown eyes, rope master, stunts,* you might find me. I can wait."

Annie bit her lip. This conversation was getting ridiculous. "I am Firecracker," she admitted. "An actor friend suggested signing up on the Catalogue just for fun, and I did. I never expected anyone to want to hire me. That is what you want, right?"

"Maybe. I promise this is nothing illegal or immoral or dodgy in any degree. My mum would approve...if she knew."

Annie digested this, biting her lip. "I don't know your mum, unless she's one of my students."

"That's unlikely. It would be easier if we could meet somewhere, and I can explain face-to-face," Spindle went on. "I'm in Windhill at present, at a friend's place. I assume you're somewhere in Sydney? The Catalogue seems to think so."

"Yes."

"Then would you nominate a neutral space where we could have a proper conversation? You can choose the day and the time and the venue. Bring a friend if you want—or pepper spray."

Annie glanced at the trees that screened the Pear Tree pub. She'd been there with Bette, but it was an odd place and maybe a bit close to home. She needed a place she rarely went.

She made up her mind. "Do you know a pub called The King's Shilling, Spindle?"

"Milson's Point? I do. I went to meet someone there a while ago."

"Another extra from the Casting Catalogue?"

"No, but it was business. I hired him, but—never mind. We can certainly get together there. When would suit you?"

"I could be there in an hour," Annie said rashly. "I've just finished work, and I'm dressed the way I am in the picture on the Catalogue."

"I'll see you there in an hour," Spindle confirmed. "I'll be the ordinary guy in the—" He broke off and apparently considered for a couple of seconds. "I'm wearing a brown sloppy-joe, though my mum suggested *Beechnuts by Bosco Boyce* is a classier term for it. Thank you for agreeing." He hung up.

Annie, wondering what exactly he thought she had agreed to, picked up the hoops and put them in her car along with the collapsible balance board, the basketball, and four pairs of stilts. She'd had to drop the music and dance component from the session because the acoustics flattened the sound, so she'd added some other activities for the more adventurous and active members as compensation.

She drove back to the eggbox studio to decant her equipment. Because she was already in her working gear, her preparations consisted of drinking a glass of the Fossmere water from Der Kaffeetanz, a splash of warm water on her face, and a comb-tidy of her hair.

After all, Spindle, whoever he was, had shopped her image looking much as she still did.

As an afterthought, she crossed the yard and told Reverie and Didymus where she was going and why.

"Not that I expect any trouble," she added.

"Would you like us to come, too?" Reverie asked. "Not to your meeting, but—"

"As your back-up singers." Didymus achieved a soft-shoe shuffle. "We could easily swing by and have a drink," he added.

"Thanks, but I'll be fine. Telling you is just a precaution. I'll have my phone. And if he's a stalker or anything, he's going an odd way about it."

"Take Debussy," Reverie suggested. "She's a grand judge of character."

"Are dogs allowed in the pub?"

"Yes. One of the barmaids is a Dame."

Annie accepted the offer and took possession of Debussy and her leash.

She was halfway to the rendezvous before she remembered Debussy's rejection of a check-up at the vet's. That hardly suggested canine perspicacity.

Oh well. Maybe it was a new vet, and she was apprehensive.

Or maybe she thought I needed to talk to her mistress, so she enticed her to the studio...

Fanciful nonsense.

She parked in a side street, not far from the fitness centre, then, accompanied by the spaniel, she walked the short distance to The King's Shilling.

She hadn't been there since the last visit she'd made with Dequan. On that occasion, she recalled, he'd been delivering a packet of information for someone. She hadn't asked about that, supposing he'd have told her if it had been any of her business. As Jezz had once remarked, he wasn't the secretive type, but he rightly minded his clients' privacy.

Annie felt a smile twitching in her cheek. She'd once thought it a pity she couldn't hire Dequan to find her a flat, but it hadn't even occurred to her to ask about a...what had Del called them? A DeDop.

The smile bloomed into a grin at the thought of his reaction if she had.

Would he have agreed? It would have been even less appropriate than asking him to source a flat.

She caught the eye of the woman behind the bar, who smiled politely before making it more personal. "Annie Blue!"

"Yes—" She looked at the woman for a few seconds before recognition fell into place. "Jumble Sayle! Where's Franco?"

"Down among my feet," Jumble said. She was barely recognisable out of her harlequin costume and make-up. "And that's Rev's Debussy. Is she with you?"

Divining that the barmaid meant the mistress rather than the dog, Annie said, "No. Debussy's just here as moral support and a canary in a coalmine." She added, "I didn't know you were a—" She hesitated.

"Barmaid or bartender is correct, but my favoured term is *alewife*," Jumble said. "It has a ring to it."

Annie smiled. "It has. I'm here to meet someone, but he didn't give his name."

"If you're using Firecracker as an alias, a chap called Spindle is waiting for you in the lounge," Jumble said. "He said whatever you order is on him." A gleam lit her eyes. "Order a bottle of Summercourt 87. I dare you."

"No, thanks. I'll have a small Treeve Perry," Annie said.

"Coming up." Jumble served it on ice. "And here's a biscuit for Debussy. It's a DWD treat, on the house."

Annie thanked her and headed for the lounge, pondering. DWD...*oh, Dames with Dogs!* She supposed it made sense that the Dames would have their own recipes for dog treats.

She reached the lounge, and, having her hands full, she allowed Debussy to nudge the door open with her nose.

She followed her in and observed the spaniel's gently waving tail and flattened ears before setting her drink and Debussy's snack on the low table.

After that, she turned her attention to Spindle, who had risen courteously from the squashy couch to greet her.

Chapter Nine: Way

Sydney May 2020

"FIRECRACKER?"

She recognised his voice and looked up, and it was a fair way up, into his face.

"Spindle."

He offered his hand. "Firecracker. Annie Blue, I think you said on the phone."

"That's right. At least, that's my business identity. My legal name is Anastasia Blugle. There won't be a spelling test with that."

"Anastasia." There was an odd tone to his voice.

"Yes. As in—"

"The Grand Duchess Anastasia."

"Right. Absolutely no relation. I was named after another grand duchess name altogether—an ancestor called Olga. She wasn't a duchess either." She stopped babbling, looking at him warily.

He'd described himself as ordinary, with brown hair and eyes. He was all that, but there was something interesting in his face, which had high cheekbones and a slightly—was it Slavic?—cast, with a broad brow and narrow chin.

Must be one of the DeDops.

She asked, "Are you reserved? As in taken, assigned, matched-up?"

"No. Are you?"

"Not currently."

Not a DeDop then. Or at least, not one of the ones Del discovered unless he's been disengaged since she hunted him down.

He gestured to the couch, and Annie sat, unclipped Debussy's leash so she could wander freely in the lounge, and offered the biscuit.

Spindle sat a polite arm's length away. "My name's Way," he said. He cleared his throat. "Wayfarer Renwin. Not a name that rolls readily off the tongue. You can blame my mother. I do. In her teens, she had a crush on a fairly obscure but undoubtedly dishy actor. Her description. When she chanced to encounter my dear old dad, who had almost reached retirement age as the bachelor bearer of one of the least common surnames known to man or woman, nothing would suit her but to marry him, produce a sprog, and match the surname with..." He turned to face her, putting out his hands in a helpless gesture. "This tale sounds less and less plausible every time I tell it. You haven't a clue what I'm talking about and why should you?"

"I expect you're named for Renwin the Wayfarer, only in reverse," Annie said.

"Exactly. You've seen the film? Mum used to have it on video, and I took her to see it on the big screen a year or so back. It was a special showing—"

"*Elven Archers of the Mist* at the Coffee Cup Ring Theatre," Annie supplied.

Spindle, or Way, flashed her a wide smile. "You saw it, too! New Year's Day. We must have ships-in-the-nighted."

"I didn't see it that night or ever," Annie said regretfully. "I was planning to go with my then boyfriend, but someone came to dinner, and it didn't happen."

"Still want to see it?" Way asked.

"That depends. Is it as corny as it looked on the poster?"

"Much, much worse," he assured. "The stars did their best with a dodgy script and shaky SFX, and my namesake-in-reverse was a real pro—the things he had that horse doing you'd swear it was CGI, which didn't exist then. I studied his scenes over and over when I was a kid."

"You had a crush on him, too?"

"No. How do they put it? I didn't want him. I wanted to *be* him. Handsome, approachable, distinguished, fair without being wishy-washy or having white rabbit eyelashes... It's down to Alain Barfleur that I got into the stunt business, though he wasn't actually a stunt man, just an actor who did his own stunts."

Alain Barfleur, Annie recalled, was the actor who played Renwin the Wayfarer. She remembered the stylised portrait on the poster, but she had no idea what the actor really looked like. He'd be quite old by now, in any case.

"Is he still working?" she asked.

"Not regularly. There was a rumour that he'd be at the screening, but it's lucky I didn't tell Mum that, because he wasn't there—not in person. He *did* appear via a big-screen recorded message, though, and talked about how much he'd enjoyed working with Hein Hoffmann and Hope Gordon—and his horse Varian, of course.

"That was enough to make Mum's evening. We had got to see him live about five years ago. He did an equestrian display at a charity event. I took Mum, and she *swooned*. I'm afraid the words *silver* and *fox* might have been deployed, along with a lot of quips about carbon copy horses. The one he was riding was the dead spit of Varian from the film. Mum started wondering about *The Picture of Varian the Steed* and whether it was kept in the attic or in the stable."

Annie cleared her throat. "Take your mum out a lot, do you?"

"If you call one major outing a year a lot. It's my perpetual Mother's Day present to her, taking her to an event of her choosing. The rest of the year, she spends her social life merry-widowing with a selection of carefully curated escorts."

Annie thought she must have shied because he held up his hand. "Not *paid* escorts. Escorts in the old-fashioned sense. She refers to them as her cicisbeos. She was married to Dad for twenty years, and I don't think she's looking for husband number two. For one thing, she'd lose the name."

He paused, smiling. "But I didn't invite you here to talk about my mum's courtiers. She's nuts, in a good way, and mostly she gets on with her life, and I get on with mine. Hers is considerably more eventful."

Annie sipped her perry. "So—why *did* you want to contact me? You're not a director, you said."

"And you're not an actor," he countered.

"As I said, my friend, who *is* an actor, got me to register in the Catalogue, just for fun."

That was sort of true, and mentioning the DeDops might have made her sound desperate or weird or even, heaven forbid, like his mum.

"What *do* you do?" he asked.

"I'm a fitness coach. I do one-on-one appointments and group sessions, trading as Annie Blue."

She put down the drink, leaped up, did a backflip, jazz hands, and announced, "Banish the blues with Annie Blue!"

Debussy gave a startled yip, then looked embarrassed.

Annie reassured her with a pat. "It's okay, Debussy. Just letting off steam." Then she sat down again.

His eyes lit up. "How do I make a booking?"

"You don't. Women only."

He gave her a disapproving look. "You can't do that. Not nowadays."

"I can, and I do. We have some little boys who come with their mums and grans, but I can't imagine any males older than ten or so wanting to participate. If we had men, they'd be outperforming the women, just through natural speed and strength." She explained Friday Fitness, Move-a-Licious, and Sparklers, and even the brief iteration of Blondin and Barnum. "That one didn't work as well as I hoped. None of my members managed more than a few steps on the rope, though a couple did learn to handle a unicycle."

He laughed. "It took me a while to master the rope, in so far as I ever have."

"What do you *want*?" Annie asked again, and more directly.

"I told you I work as a stunt performer, but I also run weekend and weekly treks and adventures. I want a female partner to come with me sometimes to make it more..." He hesitated.

"Inclusive," Annie said.

"I want women to feel secure about joining us on a climb or a hike. I don't like to contradict you, but to me it's about personal challenges, trust, and cooperation, not competition, but it's supposed to be attainable."

"Fair enough. But why me in particular?" She recalled the ersatz Annies in the Catalogue.

"Because I've been trying to find you for *years.*"

Chapter Ten: The Girl on the Tightrope

Sydney May 2020

ANNIE FOUGHT THE TEMPTATION to say *What*? or *Huh*? Instead, she just gazed at him, letting her scepticism show.

"I'm not feeding you a line," he said quickly. "Annie, do I look familiar to you at all?"

She went on looking. "You do, as it happens, but not in the usual way. This is embarrassing, probably for both of us. Don't feel obliged to take to your heels, though I'll understand if you do."

He gestured for her to go on.

"You look quite a lot like my ex. And also like a man who's engaged to my friend. If he *wasn't* taken, I'd have been interested myself."

She felt her cheeks warming and shrugged. "Told you it was embarrassing."

"You mean I'm your type."

"I don't know you, but physically, yes."

"Is that why you asked if I was—what was the word you used—assigned?"

"No. Really not. I thought you might be someone my actor friend mentioned. One of five somebodies. And they *were* all assigned. I mean—you still might be one of them. Have you been recently unassigned?"

His face lit with comprehension. "Your friend has been doing a search in the Casting Catalogue."

"Yes." Annie decided she might as well explain properly. "She and I aren't a bit alike except in one thing—we share the same ex, and we like the same *type*. She went hunting to see if she could find other representatives of that type. It was an academic exercise—not stalking. That's all."

"And she found five—but not me."

"Right. And no, she didn't contact any of them."

"She just told you about it."

"Only because we were putting my profile in the Catalogue and she was telling me how searches work. But you obviously know that."

"I do. I wonder why I didn't come up in the search."

Annie wondered, too. As she didn't know the exact terms Del had fed into the system, she couldn't even guess.

Way went on, "Leaving all that aside, I don't look familiar to you?"

Annie spread her hands. "As I said, you do, but that's because—"

"I'm your preferred type."

"We've never met before," Annie said. "I'd have remembered a name like yours." She saw him looking doubtful and said, "I met a girl named Tiffany Glockenspiel on a bus once. She had freckles. We spent about an hour talking up a storm. I've never had any other contact with her, but I remember her, plain as plain."

"You and I *have* met, though," he persisted. "We just never exchanged names." He nodded for emphasis and leaned back, absently patting Debussy, who had decided to rest against his legs. "Hello, dog. What's your name again? Gussie, was it?"

"Debussy. She belongs to my landlady."

"You're dog-sitting?"

"No, she's Annie-sitting."

He smiled at that and rubbed the spaniel's ears until she groaned with pleasure.

Still rubbing, he returned his attention to Annie. "It was back when I was twelve or so. You would have been a few years younger. Nine, maybe... Nothing?"

She shook her head. "You must be thinking of someone else."

"It was you. I've had a really strong mind picture of you all these years, just the same as you with Tiffany Glockenspiel. It happened in Darwin."

"I—" She broke off as a memory tugged at her mind.

"At a scout camp by the river."

"Oh! You're the boy who applauded me."

"And you're the girl on the tightrope. I'm *sure* you are. I hoped so when I found your profile, but from one photo taken fifteen or so years after a single meeting, it was difficult to be definite."

Annie, believing him but disbelieving the situation at large, said, "And you just happened to be looking for a tightrope walker."

"I was looking for *you,* but I've never had enough to go on. No name, no exact age, and no address. I saw you *once* in Darwin—the way you saw that girl on the bus—but the proportion of people in Darwin who weren't born there or who don't stay there is staggering."

"I've always lived in Sydney," Annie said. "I was in Darwin with my grandparents for Granny Katie's school reunion."

"I was there temporarily, too. Mum had three months' work in the territory, and while I was there, I transferred to the local Scouts via some sort of reciprocal agreement for kids of itinerant workers."

Annie nodded, remembering that day.

So that's why he didn't seem to quite fit the demographic. Like me, he didn't belong there.

"The only clues I had to identify you were the red hair, which is statistically not as common as the other colours, and what you could do, which is also not common. I also heard your grandad address you as Grand Duchess. That didn't help much. I asked Mum about it, and she said you could have been Maria or Charlotte or Tatiana or any of the female Romanovs really—she even suggested Anastasia."

Annie shook her head slowly.

"It's all true," Way said.

"I'm not doubting you. I just don't see why you would bother. I mean, I enjoyed talking to Tiffany Glockenspiel, but I've never tried to find her. She's just an...an incident."

And you were, too, she thought.

"Mum doesn't see why I bothered either," Way said. "Neither do I, but one of the chaps I hired to look into your identity said *he* understood. He'd heard of—or possibly dealt with—a couple of parallel cases. One was a woman looking for a childhood friend she used to play with. They'd exchanged names, but one day, the other child didn't come to play, and her friend never saw her again. No one else even remembered her existence.

"The other case was a woman looking for a boy she'd made a promise to when they were children. She didn't have even a first name to go on."

"That sounds impossible," Annie said. She clicked her fingers to Debussy, who rolled her eyes sideways and stayed where she was.

"It does," Way agreed. "But in both cases they had physical evidence of the other person—little gifts the other children had given them. Those helped to establish a probable culture for the mysterious identities.

"All *I* had was a memory. I even tried to contact the scoutmaster who set up the tightrope walking activity, just in case he'd met you again later at a—I don't know—some sort of tightrope walking exhibition. Hank Browning, his name was. I couldn't find him, either. According to what I did find out, he helped with the Scouts for a couple of years, then left the district and dropped out of sight. His daughter was part of the troop... Clea, or something like that. I couldn't find her, either, though I did locate a photo of her in a newspaper... Leah Downing, it said, but I'm *sure* she was Hank Browning's daughter. The name must have been a misprint."

Annie listened to that spiel on autopilot. Only one thing seemed relevant. "You actually hired someone to *look* for me? Just because you remembered me walking on a tightrope?"

"I hired two of them. They had impeccable credentials, but they didn't find you."

"I hope you got your money back."

"I did from one of them. The other one said his fees were non-refundable on the grounds that he'd put in the work. To be fair, he warned me from the outset it was probably a lost cause."

"Fair enough, I suppose. May I ask who these PIs were, exactly?"

"Not PIs. Locaters. One trades as Inkersolve. He's down the coast in Victoria. He gives a job three weeks then calls it when looking for people. He'll give it longer if it's an object. The other one is local—"

Annie flung up a hand. "I expect it's Qin-Find."

He stared at her. "So he *did* track you down? He said he couldn't help me. What did you do—offer to double his fee if you could stay lost? How unethical—though he did give my money back."

Annie started to laugh.

Way looked offended then joined in. "Okay, what's so funny?"

"Qin-Find is my ex. Either he genuinely didn't know he was looking for *me* in particular or else he *did* know or suspect it was me you wanted, and he thought it was a—what do you call it?"

"Conflict of interest? Invasion of privacy?"

"Maybe. He either didn't want to contact me or, more likely, he was trying to protect me from an obsessive stalker."

"I'm not obsessive or a stalker."

"No, but he sort of is. Obsessive, anyway, though not about me." Annie picked up her perry and drained it. Then she leaned back in the squashy couch and told Way Renwin about Dequan, about his protective cousin Lucy, and about Elfie, who traded as Elf-Made Art and who was also Dequan's long-lost first love.

"At least, I'm ninety-nine percent sure she is."

"And you haven't told him?"

"No. And it's not from spite. She knows where to find him, and, besides, she's engaged to someone else. If I told him *now* that I know where she is, he might want to know how long I've known, and, besides, it could get messy. Her fiancé works in Sydney, and she comes here quite often, so she's not *hiding*. And neither am I."

There was a bit of a pause.

Annie said, "So now you've found me when a couple of qualified investigators couldn't. Whatever made you think of looking in the Casting Catalogue for a girl you saw *once* in Darwin?"

"I thought anyone with your natural talents might have gravitated to the performing industry as a stunt performer, the way I have. I knew it was a long shot."

Annie said, "It paid off, but it easily might not have. Until this year, I hadn't walked on a tightrope since I was ten." That seemed to be that, so she changed the subject. "What you said about adventure treks, Way. Did you mean it, or was that just an excuse for luring me here?"

"What do you think?" Way gave her one of his sudden wide smiles, and she caught a flash of the friendly boy who'd admired her skill and who'd patiently helped two of the other Scouts with their acrobatics.

She smiled back. "I think you meant it, and it's something I'd very much like to do, if I can fit it into my schedule. Even if I can't, I'd love to go climbing or trekking with you sometime—for fun, not for work." She got to her feet and picked up her empty glass. "Thanks for the drink, Wayfarer Renwin."

He got up as well, gently disengaging from Debussy, who had gone to sleep leaning against his leg. "Is that a kind brush-off? If not, shall we make a day for a climb?"

"No. And yes, please. What's your schedule like?"

"Flexible when I'm not filming."

"I don't have anything on this coming Wednesday," she said.

"I can rearrange a couple of things and manage that. What sort of climb?"

"I like a bit of a challenge but nothing too technical. No hanging from a ledge by one fingertip. I'm out of practice. Something about or just above the level of Dancing Tor, say, if that's not too tame for you."

"I'd love to suggest Pigeon Tor," he said, "but that's a bit difficult to get to."

"How difficult?"

"Impractical, unless you have several weeks—shall we make it Dancing Tor then? Or how about the Pipe Organ? That's just up the coast from Parson Bay, and it's not going to be crowded."

Annie thought about the only time she'd climbed Dancing Tor. Maybe that almost perfect memory should be left to stand. "I've never done the Pipe Organ, so let's settle on that one," she said.

"Sold. Would you like me to pick you up, or would you rather travel separately?"

"I enjoy driving, so I'll pick *you* up, and you can navigate." Annie patted her phone in her pocket. "I have your number, and you have mine, so text me a pick-up point before Wednesday, and I'll swing by about seven."

"Five," he said. "That will give us time to get back for a special matinee of *Elven Archers of the Mist.*"

"Is there going to be one?"

"Depend on it."

Chapter Eleven: New Shoes

Sydney June 2020

ANNIE AND THREE OF her Sparklers had signed up to run a half marathon on Midwinter Day. One of the sponsors was Underfoot and Undefeeted, a new sports shop in Lady Lane.

It wasn't Annie's usual milieu, but she needed new running shoes and thought she'd check them out.

The cheery consultant measured her up and tested her gait, so it all took longer than she expected. She couldn't fault the system, but she reflected she'd have been able to skip straight to the try-on stage if she'd gone to her usual outlet, which had her measurements on speed-dial. It was just as well she had a couple of spare hours.

She finally emerged, wearing new shoes and carrying her old ones in a paper bag, tactfully turning down the assistant's offer of a free Underfoot tee to wear on race day. "We have team shirts already," she said, and handed over her card. "Team Annie Blue."

"Can't be shot for trying," the assistant said philosophically.

"I'll write a shoe review after the run," Annie promised.

She was turning away when she spotted a clothes shop diagonally opposite on the other side of the lane.

Fairings.

A bright arch of braided scarves attracted her attention, singing joyous harmonies of colour.

I want one.

Nonsense, Annie Blue. You don't wear scarves.

She thought wistfully of her red dress. One day, she'd wear it again.

I might have put it on to watch Elven Archers of the Mist.

She smiled at the memory.

Way had invited her to a matinee after they climbed the Pipe Organ, but she hadn't thought he was serious.

He had been.

Even then she didn't expect it to be a private showing in his mum's retro theatre.

Mum, she'd discovered, was known to the fashion world as Cossette Lacroix, niece of the legendary Judith Lacroix. Even Annie had heard of *her.*

Fortunately, the mistress of the house was out of the country, so Annie had been able to enjoy the guilty pleasure of watching elves in tunics, cloaks, sweeping tresses, and winged brows to the full without worrying too much whether she'd got popcorn in her cleavage or was laughing too loudly at the most blatant anachronisms in the dialogue and the even more blatant sideways smoulders of the two leads.

"Just exactly what was your mum doing in Darwin back then?" she asked Way as he poked about in the fridge during the interval.

It was a long film, and she was glad to get up from the designer cinema chair and stretch her legs.

"Working," he said glibly. "Carrots, cucumber, celery, radishes?"

"All of the above. As?"

"She had a three-month *Evolutions* shoot." He pulled out a wedge of scary orange cheese.

"*Evolutions...*"

"Darwin's theory of," he said, and added, "What that has to do with high-end fashion is anyone's guess. Mum's mind works in mysterious ways."

Annie picked up a knife and started slicing a giant green apple he'd plonked on a plate. "When you called me, you said you were staying with a friend."

"I said I was at a friend's place, and so I was. Dion le Fay—we were at school together for a few months."

"Le Fay... Anything to do with the Fairy Gardens people?"

"Not him personally, but his family founded it. Why?"

"You're slippery," she said, shaking her head.

"I'm really not." He looked downcast for a moment. "Annie, if you ever think I'm not being straightforward, call me on it. I sometimes slide around the point, but it's not intentional. It's habit. The term *nepo baby* doesn't appeal to me or to Mum, so I generally don't advertise what she does for a living."

"Okay," she said.

"Okay what?"

"I will call you on it. And it you think I'm being too much *in your face* or if I start bouncing about like the electric chimp and embarrassing you in public, you tell me."

"Deal." He handed her the plate of vegetables. "Let's watch the rest of the film."

Annie said, "Yes. I want to see what that horse will do next. I get that the flying scenes are rigged with wires and harnesses, but however did they do the *horse?*"

"That was one thing I hoped to find out from Alain Barfleur when I saw him doing the display, but it wasn't a question he wanted to answer."

"Trade secret, I expect. He was—impressive."

"My mum was *very* impressed," he said. "If she hadn't been incognito in a cowgirl hat, she'd probably have asked him for a selfie."

Still smiling over the memory of the film and the interval conversation, though regretting the red dress a bit, Annie was about to walk on when she saw several women approaching Fairings from the other direction.

She recognised one of them as Dahlia Pengellis, the accountant who had recommended her to her solicitor. She was with a handsome older woman dressed in jewel blue. Annie was fairly sure it was the solicitor's wife whom she had met at his office. Another was Nell Andover, easily identifiable by the baby sling containing her old chihuahua. It was the fourth familiar face that stopped Annie in her tracks. Elfie, or rather Tamzin, was hurrying towards the others, who greeted her with obvious delight.

They all entered the shop under cover of a musical tinkle that seemed to Annie to be playing a tune.

On impulse, she crossed the lane and entered the shop in their wake.

Elfie was being fitted for her wedding dress.

She greeted Annie as cordially as if she'd been an invited guest, and Annie watched, with her usual feeling of mixed delight and envy, as her displaced angel was ceremoniously arrayed in a long green tunic covered with a floating overlay of colours.

A party in a gown. How very unbridely. How very Elfie.

Annie smiled, exclaimed, admired, and surfed the waves of goodwill and friendship.

I'm part of this. This vibe is what I bring to Move-a-Licious and Friday Fairy Fitness... I bring women together in friendship and hope.

Elfie twirled on the designer's command, then stopped suddenly and got a phone out of her bag. She caught Annie's eye and beckoned.

"Annie...would you? My oldest friend isn't here, and I don't think she'll be able to come to the wedding at such short notice, even though I'll invite her. I'd love to share this moment with her."

Annie nodded and watched while Elfie contacted her old friend, explained the situation, then handed the phone over.

Annie backed away, and turned on the video function, panning over the bride-to-be from her head to her shoes. She'd noticed those shoes before, because Elfie wore them habitually. The heels had a swirling pattern of colour that somehow echoed the dress, the ring, and a delightful matching bracelet.

Annie handed back the phone and looked down at her feet in their bright new running shoes. The blazing whiteness blurred a little.

This is me. I'm the woman in the running clothes. I'm not the one in the most beautiful dress in the world. I'm not the one who walks in sunlight and dances on love and seems to remember some lost paradise.

I never will be.

Then—she smiled. Because the woman in running clothes wasn't *all* she was.

She was also the girl on the tightrope.

Chapter Twelve: Plus One

Sydney June 2020

THE FITTING WAS SOMETHING of a complicated whirlwind, not only for the virtual attendance of Elfie's old friend, but also regarding a woman with greying brown hair and a hippy costume who blew in and had a minor confrontation with the embroiderer who was helping arrange Elfie's hair. She called Elfie by yet another name, said something cutting about elves and something someone had done to someone called Wayne, gifted Elfie with a pair of gold hoop earrings, bought a blouse, and breezed out again.

Annie was fascinated, but none of the other women seemed ruffled by the disturbance. By then, she had tentatively identified one of them as another Dame—the one with the border collie—and two more as Matin's mother and sister. She supposed they were all somehow used to disturbances and took them in their stride.

As the only one out of the loop, she cornered Elfie and asked for an explanation.

"Whatever is going on? Who was she? Why did she call you Abbie? Who's Wayne? And what elf man have you got, and what did he do to Wayne?"

Elfie brushed back her wavy hair, making her betrothal ring flash with coloured light and said, with smiling apology, "It's such a very, very long story, Annie. You probably won't believe it, but remind me to tell you sometime, preferably after the wedding."

"I will," Annie said, smiling back. "I hope you and Matin have a lovely day and a lovely life together."

"We shall...and we both hope you'll come along to celebrate with us. We're holding the ceremony in the Fairy Gardens at the chapel. That's near where you have some of your sessions, right?"

Annie nodded.

"It's on the fourteenth, at two o'clock at the little chapel. We only just decided a few days ago. Do please come."

"I will," Annie said.

"And bring a plus one or a friend if you want. It's all informal."

Annie nodded, and Elfie reached out and grasped both her hands in friendship before whirling away to change into her ordinary clothes, a displaced angel no more.

Annie, curiously elated, ran back up Lady Lane to where she'd left her car.

With a feeling of inevitability, she saw Way propped against the bonnet, smiling as she approached.

"What are you doing here?" Annie enquired, dropping her old shoes in the back of the car and accepting his warm hug.

"Waiting for you, my Annie Blue," he said into her hair. "It's been a long time."

"Only a day or so."

"Only fifteen years."

That felt confronting, so she sidestepped and said, "Weren't you supposed to be dangling from a ledge somewhere today, making Mac Doran look good?"

"Yes, but not until this afternoon. I have the fourteenth free if you want to come roller skating at the new RollerBowl. They're doing interior shots that day and won't need me."

Annie felt a stab of regret. "I would have liked to, but I'm going to a wedding. You remember when I told you about Elfie?"

"The sweetheart who used to belong to Qin-Find?"

"At least five of us come into that category," she said drily. "And one of us went there twice. But yes, Elfie was the first of us, and ultimately she was the reason I moved on. *Not* her fault or Qin-Find's. Just—"

"Obsessions with first loves are dangerous things," he said. "That's why I would never admit to one, even to myself."

"Lucky for you," Annie said. She added, "You *could* come to the wedding as my plus one if you're willing to raincheck the skating. It's informal, and we could always RollerBowl afterwards. Is there an evening session?"

"We could, but are you wearing your running things to the wedding?"

She frowned. "No. I'm sure it's not *that* informal."

"What are you wearing then? Is it suitable for skating in?"

"I'll probably wear a red dress my friend Jezz designed for me—unless I go mad and buy something frilly from Fairings."

She waited for him to say something about the inadvisability of Annie Blue wearing something frilly.

Instead, he said, "I hope whatever you choose to wear will go with this." He opened the car, tossed his phone into the console and unzipped the diagonal pocket in his pullover. It was steel blue with a rolled down collar. Annie wondered if it was another Bosco Boyce design, but before she could ask, he pulled out a fine gold chain and offered it in his closed fist.

She allowed him to drop it into her palm and looked speechlessly at the gemstone clasped in the centre of the chain. It looked like a star sapphire with different colours radiating in sparks and rays from a clear centre. It couldn't possibly be real.

"What is that?" Her voice, when it finally consented to work, sounded distant in her ears.

Way looked nonplussed. "It's a drop pendant. Someone Mum knows set it for me... Lawrence Goldsmith. He's mostly retired, but he does work occasionally for people he likes. For some reason he likes Mum. *Likes* her, I mean. He's not one of her cicisbeos."

Annie recalled the name. That was surely the man who had looked into the provenance of the opal ring Grandad Petre had found.

Webs.

"I mean—what's the stone? *Is* it a stone? A natural one? Or is it cloisonne or...or something? It's lovely, whatever it is."

Her mind scrambled about in the chunky little book she'd found and failed to see a match.

"It's a prism stone. I picked it up on an island a long time ago and had it polished and set just recently."

"I've never seen anything like it before!"

"I'm not surprised. In the rough they look like dust-coloured pebbles, but if you dip one in water or put it in your mouth then hold it up to the sun the colours come dimly through. Naturally, you have to be careful not to swallow it.

"When you polish it you get something unique—and I mean that precisely. One of the locals told me no two will ever be the same. I collected a standard pocketful, which is allowable. Any more is considered greedy. This is the one I liked best..."

Uncharacteristically, he let his words trail off.

Annie lifted the chain and let the stone shimmer and spin, darting colours and stirring memories.

A party in a stone.

"Why?" she managed, mesmerised.

"It reminds me of you. The way I saw it, I could either keep it to look at in my old age and remember my sparkling girl on a tightrope, or else I could find you and give it to you. No expectations. No strings. No promises...but it's yours. So am I, of course, if you want me, but that was never a condition. You might have been—what did you call it? Reserved? Or assigned? Or just plain not liked the cut of my jib."

Annie said, "I love it, and I'll treasure it forever. As for you—the jury is out. I don't suppose you have a red shirt to wear to the wedding?"

"Ours?"

She stared him down.

"Too soon?"

"Much too soon. Give it...I don't know... a few days?"

He laughed, as she intended. "I don't own a red shirt, but I'm sure I can rustle up something appropriate."

"It will have to be something that can live up to being the plus one of a woman wearing a party in a stone."

"Tall order."

"You could always ask your mum to pick something out."

"Nonsense. I've been choosing my own clothes since I was twelve."

Annie laughed. "I'll meet you at the Fairy Gardens at one-thirty on the fourteenth then, wearing a shirt *not* chosen by your mum."

"I was hoping we might go hiking tomorrow to Sapphire Gorge. It's a Grade Four hike—half an hour from Mum's place. Two hours in, two hours out, and an hour at the bottom to rest and recuperate and cool our feet in the coldest liquid water you can imagine. Believe me, we'll need it."

"I'm training with my team for a half marathon in the morning."

He looked disappointed, but he gave a philosophical smile. "Another time then."

"But," Annie said, "I could manage in the afternoon."

Epilogue: New Year's Eve

Sydney NYE 2021

ANNIE AND WAY ARRIVED at the Fairy Gardens at eight o'clock on the last day of the old year. It was still daylight, but lanterns glowed palely through the trees, and the music was already getting lively.

"The others are probably here already," Annie said.

Way gave her a one-armed hug. "Want me to make myself scarce around midnight? I don't want to impinge on your girlfriend tradition."

"You won't. I expect Del will have her latest in tow."

"Remind me to give her a kiss."

"Why?" Annie tugged him to a stop, surprisingly displeased.

"For talking you into signing up for the Catalogue, obviously. I wouldn't have found you otherwise."

"How do you know that was Del? *I* never told you."

"No, you were always careful to say *an actor friend*, but she's the only candidate I can think of. I won't talk about it to anyone else."

"Except your mum. I bet she was all over the story."

"You've got to admit it's a good one. Me using logic to track down and get the girl. Mum's opinion of me went up no end. I never mentioned your friend's role to her, though. I let her think you just signed up in the extra listing because—because it was the sort of thing you'd do."

Annie gave in. "All right. It was Del." She added, "I suppose Puck might bring Mister Puck."

"I expect Puck will. Schmoozing with your girlfriends on New Year's Eve while leaving a husband of five minutes to languish isn't a good look."

A PARTY IN A STONE

"Five months."

"Near enough."

Mister Puck was properly called Joop Niemandsverdriet, but Annie had never even attempted to say that aloud.

Puck Verhoven had joined the Three Flees, which immediately, so Del said, translated them into the Quad Squad the year before.

December 2020

Puck and Dequan had broken up in mid-December, and Del, whose finger was firmly on the pulse of any gossip, had promptly introduced herself to the understandably startled Dutchwoman and invited her to spend New Year's Eve 2020 dancing among the fairy lights with the rest of the Dequan Discards.

According to Del, Puck had looked bemused but had agreed and, after the first cautious half hour when it had been made clear to her that despite Del's comment, Dequan was someone they were all fond of in absentia, she warmed to the occasion.

"I shall miss him," she said, examining the toes of her elegant shoes.

"We all do, up to a point," Jezz said. "Though not me so much. These days we're quite good friends."

Annie saw that Jezz was gazing at Puck as a cat might gaze at a particularly luscious pigeon and laid a bet with herself that Puck would soon be having her measurements taken for a custom gown.

Jezz did that if she happened to like you.

"Karaoke for four!" Del announced and towed the others towards the MC.

Annie, who had just spotted Way heading in their direction, resisted, but Del prevailed, and soon had them crowded around the single mic.

"I got their backs an' they got mine," she began, singing slowly.

She paused, looking about, then blew a kiss to the crowd.

"Girlfriends!" She smiled and drawled, *"We got time!"*

Annie, relaxing, joined in with the nonsense lyrics as backing.

"Doo-doo-doopy-doo! Girlfriends! We got time!"

It was the silliest song, but the music was upbeat, and Del was selling it, dancing in her trademark white dress.

"Men don't know what they're missin'!
Girlfriends! No need for kissin'!
Got my back
And that's
The way it be!
No man can ever come twixt
My girlfriends...
And me!"

"Doo-doo-doopy-doo!" Annie hummed.

"My girlfriends... They got my back! My girlfriends..."

Del let the song fade out, then yelled, "Let's hear it for my girlfriends, Annie Blue of Annie Blue Fitness, who taught me to do a cartwheel, Jezz Finchley of Jezz Finchley Fashion, who designed my fabulous dress tonight, and Puck Verhoven of—" She paused and glanced enquiringly at Puck who laughed suddenly and said, "Chemist for Tulip Town Perfumery."

"—who joined us tonight for the very first time!" Del said.

That brought a somewhat disconcerted silence from the crowd of dancers, but someone started applauding.

That broke the ice, and Annie was unsurprised to realise it was Way.

He was beaming at them as proudly as if they'd been his little sisters. "Go, girlfriends!" he yelled.

It was all so silly...but that, Annie realised later, was the point when she decided to marry him. He'd mentioned it a few times, just tossing the idea into the conversation, but Annie had been waiting for the other shoe to drop.

Now, in this moment, she allowed herself to believe it wouldn't.

Renwin. The name was just as rare as Blugle, if not more so, but at least it was easy to spell.

A PARTY IN A STONE

She'd been willing to take on Qin, after all.

They all bowed, and Del relinquished the microphone to four young men who were so alike they must be brothers.

"Tasty," Del said audibly, and one of the boys laughed nervously.

"It's okay. You're too young for me," she assured him, and they went to meet Way.

NYE 2021

Remembering that evening a year later, on the verge of 2022, Annie wondered how, and even if, their girlfriends tradition could continue.

Puck, as Way pointed out, was married, Del had acquired a musician, Jezz—she wasn't sure—and Annie herself was engaged.

How could a group of assorted women whose connection was a joint ex remain close as they moved on into their separate futures?

She looked down affectionately at her engagement ring. It was another prism gem...*a party in a stone*. On her other hand, she wore the gold-and-opal ring Grandad Pete had promised her years ago. He had met Way and approved, and the conversation had moved to metal detecting. That had reminded Pete of the ring, which in turn had reminded him of his promise to Anastasia.

"Not an engagement ring—reckon Way will see to that—just something nice to wear sometimes," he'd said.

Annie had slid it on to her right hand.

"Very nice, Grand Duchess," Pete had said.

To her that hath shall be given...

"There they are," Way said, indicating a small group near the little chapel. He paused. "There seem to be more of you this year... Qin-Find *has* been busy."

Annie squinted through the wavering light of the lanterns.

There were Jezz and Del, and Puck in a dark pink dress whose severe lines offset her natural elegance, but there were others with them.

As she watched, a small woman in green, holding a toddler in her arms turned and inclined her head.

"Lucy!" Annie said. She tugged Way to a stop. "That's Lucy Tan! Dequan's cousin."

Another woman, also dressed in green and also holding a small child, turned as Lucy had to smile at Annie and Way. She handed the child to her tall, brown-haired companion and came to meet Annie.

"Jezz said you'd be here soon."

"Elfie? What are you doing here?" It was a less-than-graceful greeting, but having Elfie anywhere near Lucy Tan seemed a bad idea. Lucy blamed Elfie for Dequan's commitment problems even more than Annie had.

"I'm playing a guest set," Elfie said, unhitching her violin from her back. She smiled up at Way. "Annie's plus one from our wedding, if I'm not mistaken."

"Wayfarer Renwin," Annie said. "Named for a character in a film."

Too late, she remembered how that film had to do with elves and how that— She broke off. That was ridiculous. She couldn't even remember why that might be significant.

"We're engaged," Way said cheerfully, sliding his arm around Annie.

"Lovely." Elfie looked him over. "Brown hair, check, tall, check, good looking, check—made to order for our Annie."

"Which is lucky for me."

"I'm so pleased for you both."

Lucy came over and stood by Elfie, barely reaching her shoulder. "Hello again, Anastasia. I see you know Tamzin already."

"Yes, but—"

"Annie is one of my clients. She knows me as Elf-Made Art, or Elfie," Elfie said diplomatically.

Lucy narrowed her eyes, and said, "Mmm-hmm." Her baby babbled something, and Lucy softened. "This is Mayflower Blarney-Tan," she said. "She's been getting acquainted with Tam and Matin's Music." She indicated the child in Matin Campania's arms.

Jezz came over, smiling. "Hi, Annie, Way. I see you're getting caught up on the news. Tam and I were at school together, and until a few days ago, I had no idea she was back in the country." She looked about and indicated a tall young man—or maybe a boy—who had turned to look at them. "That's Ro Folly, by the way. He's—"

"Here with Jezz," the man said in a much deeper voice than Annie expected.

Annie couldn't help staring. Here was yet another man with brown hair and *that* look. He could have passed as Way's much younger brother.

He caught her eye. "I know I don't look it, but I was born plonk in the middle of Gen Y," he said, grinning. "But it might be worse. My grandad looks younger than Dad."

"Hello," Annie said and glanced at Jezz.

Jezz! Really?

"Ro, go and look after Mister Puck," Jezz ordered him. "He's looking lost. And take Way with you—and Del's musician if you can find him. Lucy—have you got a man floating about here? If so, Ro can take him off our hands, too."

"Jack's here somewhere, but he's not mine. He's Mayflower's grandad, and I might need him to wrangle Mayflower," Lucy said.

"That seems to be my cue," Way said equably. He kissed Annie. "I'll be back to count the new year in," he promised and went off with Jezz's slave.

Annie watched them go. "Where did you find *him*, Jezz? And what *is* going on?"

Jezz said, "*He* found *me*. Came in to pick up a dress I did for his sister—her name's Altansarnai if you can believe that—and he invited me out for a drink. I laughed at him. He flashed his driver's licence to prove he was legal and looked hangdog. That made me feel—oh, you don't need to know the tedious details. As for what's going on, it's a debriefing of sorts. Sorry I didn't give you a heads up, Annie, but I had no idea if I was going to pull this off. Rodas helped with the logistics. He's a statistician." She reached out to Elfie. "I hope—"

"It's fine," Elfie said. "Matin knows all about my unfortunate obsession with...what does Delphine call him?"

"Dequan the Discarder," Jezz said in a dry voice. "But she acknowledged that that's totally unfair."

"I know it's partly my fault," Elfie said. "Believe me, I would have been in touch to tell him what was going on if I could. It wasn't possible—well, that was what I genuinely believed."

"You came back a while ago, though," Annie said.

"Yes, I did, back in twenty-seventeen. I fully intended to get in touch with him, and I did go to his flat but—" She shrugged ruefully.

"You saw him with me," Annie said.

Elfie went on looking at her. "I have occasionally wondered if you saw me—knew me—that day. It seemed so unlikely."

"I recognised you from your photos on Dequan's life-board," Annie admitted. "I used to look at them while I was waiting for the toaster."

"So why didn't you say anything when we met at my studio?"

"I wasn't sure and—it was your business. Besides, how would I have gone to my boyfriend and said, *by the way, your first girlfriend saw us going for a run, but she hasn't come to see you—*?"

"I see that, and, yes, it was my business and my responsibility to explain. I could, and should, have handled it much better than I did." Elfie sighed. "If you remember, I promised you the full story after our wedding, but we've never actually acted on that promise. Maybe the time has come. Not tonight, but soon."

"We could meet at Der Kaffeetanz next week," Annie said.

"Yes, why not." Elfie looked at the others. "Lucy, you know most of it, but Jezz, you and—" She looked enquiringly at Puck.

"My name is Puck, and Delphine, you know."

"Not really, but her, too—you come along and bring anyone else who needs the round tale. I do warn you it will sound unbelievable—except maybe to you, Lucy."

"I believe it, *liebchen*," a quiet voice said from behind Annie.

She swivelled to see a serene-looking woman with glossy chestnut hair in a milkmaid braid. She held out her hand. "Martina Qin, *liebling*. You are Stace, I think? Tamzin, I know, but not you others."

Elfie smiled warmly and hugged the woman. "Tina! I didn't know you were coming!"

"We had Christmas with Dequan's family," the woman said. "My nieces and Yanick are looking after Fee Kaffee—my café, you know." She grimaced. "After last year's escapade, they owe me."

"Dequan's here, as well, then," Elfie said, stepping back. "May—"

The microphone roared and squealed, and the compare came on line.

"Please welcome Tamzin Campania with *New Year Polka*."

"That's my cue," Elfie said and headed for the makeshift stage, beginning to play as she went.

Jezz sighed. "I get some of you corralled, and now one runs off. Why *is* it so difficult to get everyone together?"

"I have often asked myself this," Martina Qin said. "My nieces—there are two of them, but they can be in four different places at once, and Yanick disappears into the larder." She clicked her tongue.

Annie was staring at her still.

"There you are, *fraulein*!"

Jezz threw up her hands. "Deq, you're late. Tam was here, but now she's not. It's like trying to herd flipping cats!"

"Settle down, Jezz." Dequan patted her shoulder, slid an arm around Martina, then looked ruefully at the rest of them.

"This seems less and less of a good idea, but the logistics of getting you all together a second time would be even worse. Once Tam's done her set—hello, Puck. I meant to thank you for the advice you gave me—as you see, I took it." He looked down at Martina.

His *wife*? Annie thought in dazed disbelief.

Engaged, as she was, to a man who loved climbing, scrambling, and exploring as much as she did, she still found room for a touch of chagrin as she looked at the woman who had mended whatever was wrong with Dequan Qin.

She was handsome, buxom, with a wholesome glow to her that reminded Annie of Riva Bless. Even her accent was similar. She looked nothing like Elfie or Delphine or Annie herself or Puck or Jezz—and yet she *was* his type.

She said, aloud, almost without thinking, "Dequan, did it ever occur to you that we girlfriends look like a chocolate box assortment?"

He looked puzzled and glanced down at his latest...no, his *last,* if Annie was any judge. "No—"

"But *yes, liebling*!" Martina said with enthusiasm. "Just so! We must all pose together, and you will take our photo, and Tamzin will turn us into a handsome portrait to hang above our bed."

"That sounds to me an excellent idea," Puck said. "Dequan will like that, I think."

Dequan looked—appalled.

Annie reached out and patted his cheek. "Happy New Year, Qin-Find. I'm glad you gave Way his money back when you couldn't or wouldn't locate me. Which was it, by the way?"

"Er—wouldn't," he muttered.

"That must have hurt your professional pride, but thanks anyway." Then she started to laugh.

A PARTY IN A STONE

Afterword: The people at the NYE party.
The girlfriends – and Lucy – and their entourage

ANASTASIA BLUGLE/ANNIE Blue is a compact and athletic redhead and a fitness instructor. Ex-girlfriend of Dequan Qin and now fiancée of Wayfarer Renwin. Annie previously appeared in *Being Tamzin*.

Delphine DiConti is dark, dramatic, and curvy. She is an actor. Ex-girlfriend of Dequan Qin and currently has a musician in tow.

Elfie/Tamzin Campania is slender with wavy brown hair. She's an artist and musician and stars in the *Being Tamzin* series. She also appears in *Performing Pippin Pearmain* and is referred to in the *Counterpoint* series and *Geese a Laying*. Ex-girlfriend of Dequan Qin, wife of Matin Campania, and mother of Music Campania.

Jezz Finchley, who organised the gathering, is a broad-shouldered blonde dress designer. Jezz appears in *Being Tamzin* and in *Geese a Laying*. Ex-girlfriend of Dequan Qin and current owner, so to speak, of Rodas Folly.

Lucy Blarney-Tan is Dequan's cousin. She is, in her own words, small and mostly Chinese. She works as a Camp Companion for the Vouch-Safe company. Lucy stars in *Queen of the May* and appears in *Being Tamzin, The Pear Tree* and *Geese a Laying*. She is married to Paris Blarney and is the mother of Mayflower Blarney-Tan. Like her cousin, she has a courtfolk ancestor.

Martina Bless Qin is chestnut-haired with a broad forehead. She is an alpenfee and a café owner. Wife of Deqan Qin. Martina appears in *Geese a Laying, Being Tamzin, Just Eloped,* and the *Counterpoint* series.

Puck Verhoven Niemandsverdriet is a tall and elegant blonde Dutchwoman. She works as a perfume chemist for Tulip Town Perfumery. She is an ex-girlfriend of Dequan and is married to Mister

Puck—Joop Niemandsverdriet. Puck appears in *Being Tamzin* and *Geese a Laying.*

The Men

Dequan Qin, cousin of Lucy, ex of Tamzin, Jezz, Del, Annie, and Puck, and husband of Martina is tall and blond/brown-haired. He runs Qin-Find. Dequan is mostly human with a Dutch Australian Mother, a Chinese Australian father, and a distant courtfolk ancestor. He appears in *Being Tamzin, Geese a Laying, Just Eloped, Queen of the May,* and *Performing Pippin Pearmain.*

Matin Campania is tall and brown-haired. He works for Wildwood Studio and later co-owns Arts in Tune. He is Tamzin's husband and Music's father. Matin appears in *Being Tamzin* and *Performing Pippin Pearmain.* Matin in an elf. So is his colleague, Garret Rosebay, which accounts for Tezza Wilde's quip when Annie saw them near Pitons on Ice.

Mister Puck, aka Joop Niemandsverdriet, is tall and blond/brown-haired. He is Dutch. He's Puck's old family friend turned husband. Occupation unknown.

Paris Blarney is Lucy's man. He's not present at the gathering, because he is half waterfolk and seldom comes humanside. His human dad, Jack Blarney Miller, is somewhere in the crowd. Paris appears in *Queen of the May, Being Tamzin,* the *Counterpoint* series, and *Love Began at Christmas.* Jack appears in several books, including the *Cream Man* series.

Rodas Folly is tall and brown-haired and youthful-looking. He's Jezz's self-appointed slave. He's a grandson of John Folly through his son William, which accounts for his unusual appearance. He's mostly human but has enough sylvan blood to affect his looks and his rate of ageing. He works as a statistician.

Wayfarer Renwin is a stunt performer and trek leader. He is tall and brown-haired with a Slavic cast to his features. He's Annie's fiancé. As for *what* he is, he hasn't explained that yet, but it's pretty certain he's not entirely human.

Alain Barfleur is mentioned several times, although he never appears. Alain is a courtfolk man and a Flaxen Knight. He has worked occasionally as an actor over the years but spends most of his time at home on Flaxen Isle. Alain is around seventy. He has lately reconnected with Pippin Pearmain, with whom he worked in a film when he was nineteen, and is making the most of his silver years romance.

Babies:

Mayflower Blarney-Tan, Lucy's daughter, born February 2021. Mayflower is almost three-quarters human.

Music Campania, Tamzin and Matin's daughter, born March 2021. Music is a straight halfling.

Easter Eggs

THE FOUR YOUNG MUSICIANS Del disconcerted on NYE 2020 are the four Merriweather boys from *Sam and the Sylvan* as well as other titles.

Leah Downing/Cleo Browning was, in fact, Tamzin "Elfie" Herrick—so she and Way would have known one another as children. However, her iteration as Cleo was marked by anger and sulkiness, because her parents had dragged her away from her friend, Emily, and refused to let her explain, so she wouldn't have befriended Way.

Hank Browning, the scout leader who could walk the tightrope, was Tamzin's father under his Darwin identity. His real name is Paul Bysshe-Minister. This is explored in *Being Tamzin* and *Performing Pippin Pearmain*.

The woman who ambushes Tamzin's wedding dress fitting is her mother. Adelie Spenser has used a great many aliases in her time, but the one she channels during that encounter is Ashley Stevenson, whom she *became* when her daughter was about seven. Tamzin's name then was Abbie.

The film Anastasia saw part of with her grandad and which she tried to identify through the Casting Catalogue is *Dingo Nights,* starring Pippin Pearmain from the *Performing Pippin Pearmain* series.

Alain Barfleur and his horse, Varian, are a bit of an obsession with Way's mum. She and Way refer to *carbon copy steeds* and equate Varian with *The Picture of Dorian Gray.* Varian is, in fact, the same age as Alain and will live happily on while Alain does. This is explained in *Performing Pippin Pearmain.*

John Folly House, where Way has done a bit of directing, is the college Dame Billie Clarty and her friends attended in *The Theatrical Sigh.*

The two cases of people looking for people they hadn't seen in a long time that Way mentions are from *I Promise* and *Floribunda and the Best Men.* The second locator is Duffy Inkersoll from *Pen and Ink, Pisky Business* and *Man Overboard.*

It was the early encounter with Way that shaped Annie's taste for men who looked like him.

By the way, I did mention the fantasy elements are very lowkey in this story. Did you spot any? There's the matter of Varian, Alain Barfleur's horse, who is indeed still living at roughly seventy years old. Then there's the leash Reverie Eden suddenly has when she comes to lure Debussy out from under Annie's bed, and Jodiel's quip about her being a fairy godmother. Jodiel was being serious! Since Jodiel is Didymus' niece, she is not blood-connected with Reverie. Reverie also offered to *glamour it down* if her hymn-singing was too loud. This is a reference to a fairy glamour. Skyside, where Matin Campania was born, is *over there* in the fay homeland. That's why he's shifty about mentioning it. It's also why Tamzin was dishevelled when Annie encountered her at Fiddler's Rest. She and Matin had just returned from Skyside and had got wet on the way. A few of the characters in this story are at least partly fay. Matin and his colleague Garret Rosebay are elves and Martina Qin and Riva Bless are alpenfee—fairies aligned with the alplands *over there*. Some of the others are part or wholly courtfolk—fairies aligned with the courtlands and with France.

About the Author

LARK WESTERLY LIVES in Tasmania, where she walks dogs and weaves her stories on a daily basis.

She is the author of more books than she can remember. Most of these are listed on her website at https://larksinger.weebly.com

www.ingramcontent.com/pod-product-compliance
Lightning Source LLC
Chambersburg PA
CBHW072124170626
46813CB00004B/1683